Dragon Kiss

Also From Donna Grant

Don't miss these other spellbinding novels!

Dragon King Series
Dragon Revealed
Dragon Mine
Dragon Unbound
Dragon Eternal
Dragon Lover
Dragon Arisen
Ignite the Magic (prequel story)
Dragon Frost

Reaper Series
Dark Alpha's Claim
Dark Alpha's Embrace
Dark Alpha's Demand
Dark Alpha's Lover
Tall Dark Deadly Alpha Bundle
Dark Alpha's Night
Dark Alpha's Hunger
Dark Alpha's Awakening
Dark Alpha's Redemption
Dark Alpha's Temptation
Dark Alpha's Caress
Dark Alpha's Obsession
Dark Alpha's Need
Dark Alpha's Silent Night
Dark Alpha's Passion
Dark Alpha's Command
Dark Alpha's Fury

Skye Druid Series
Iron Ember
Shoulder the Skye
Heart of Glass

Kindred: The Fated Series
Rage

Ruin
Reign

Dark King Series
Dark Heat (3 novella compilation)
Darkest Flame
Fire Rising
Burning Desire
Hot Blooded
Night's Blaze
Soul Scorched
Dragon King (novella)
Passion Ignites
Smoldering Hunger
Smoke And Fire
Dragon Fever (novella)
Firestorm
Blaze
Dragon Burn (novella)
Heat
Torched
Dragon Night (novella)
Dragonfire
Dragon Claimed (novella)
Ignite
Fever
Dragon Lost (novella)
Flame
Inferno
Whisky and Wishes (novella)
Heart of Gold (novella)
Of Fire and Flame (novella)
A Dragon's Tale (novella compilation)
My Fiery Valentine

Kindred Series
Everkin
Eversong
Everwylde
Everbound

Evernight
Everspell

Dark Warrior Series
Midnight's Master
Midnight's Lover
Midnight's Seduction
Midnight's Warrior
Midnight's Kiss
Midnight's Captive
Midnight's Temptation
Midnight's Promise
Midnight's Surrender (novella)
A Warrior for Christmas

Dark Sword Series
Dangerous Highlander
Forbidden Highlander
Wicked Highlander
Untamed Highlander
Shadow Highlander
Darkest Highlander

Rogues of Scotland Series
The Craving
The Hunger
The Tempted
The Seduced

Chiasson Series
Wild Fever
Wild Dream
Wild Need
Wild Flame
Wild Rapture

LaRue Series
Moon Kissed
Moon Thrall
Moon Bound

Moon Struck

Shield Series
A Dark Guardian
A Kind of Magic
A Dark Seduction
A Forbidden Temptation
A Warrior's Heart

Druids Glen Series
Highland Mist
Highland Nights
Highland Dawn
Highland Fires
Highland Magic
Mystic Trinity (connected)

Sisters of Magic Trilogy
Shadow Magic
Echoes of Magic
Dangerous Magic

Sons of Texas Series
The Hero
The Protector
The Legend
The Defender
The Guardian

Heart of Texas Series
The Christmas Cowboy Hero
Cowboy, Cross My Heart
My Favorite Cowboy
A Cowboy Like You
Looking for a Cowboy
A Cowboy Kind of Love

Standalone Cowboy Novels
Home for a Cowboy Christmas
That Cowboy of Mine

Dragon Kiss

A Dragon Kings Novella

By Donna Grant

1001 DARK NIGHTS
PRESS

Dragon Kiss
A Dragon Kings Novella
By Donna Grant

1001 Dark Nights
Copyright 2024 Donna Grant
ISBN: 979-8-88542-052-5

Foreword: Copyright 2014 M. J. Rose

Published by 1001 Dark Nights Press, an imprint of Evil Eye Concepts, Incorporated

Acknowledgments from the Author

To MJ, Liz, and Jillian, you ladies are the best. Thank you for loving books and creating such an amazing publishing company that I'm proud to be a part of. A special thanks to everyone involved in the publishing process. You all rock!

I need to send a shoutout to the BETA readers who keep everything straight in the my ever-growing Dark Universe. Without you and your meticulous notes, you keep me from forgetting the smaller things. And some of the big ones.

To my ARC-Angels. Thank you for always being ready and willing to read over the ARCs and get reviews up on release day. You guys are the best!

And to all my readers—thank you. I wouldn't be able to share my worlds without you.

One Thousand and One Dark Nights

Once upon a time, in the future…

*I was a student fascinated with stories and learning.
I studied philosophy, poetry, history, the occult, and
the art and science of love and magic. I had a vast
library at my father's home and collected thousands
of volumes of fantastic tales.*

*I learned all about ancient races and bygone
times. About myths and legends and dreams of all
people through the millennium. And the more I read
the stronger my imagination grew until I discovered
that I was able to travel into the stories... to actually
become part of them.*

*I wish I could say that I listened to my teacher
and respected my gift, as I ought to have. If I had, I
would not be telling you this tale now.
But I was foolhardy and confused, showing off
with bravery.*

*One afternoon, curious about the myth of the
Arabian Nights, I traveled back to ancient Persia to
see for myself if it was true that every day Shahryar
(Persian: شهريار, "king") married a new virgin, and then
sent yesterday's wife to be beheaded. It was written
and I had read that by the time he met Scheherazade,
the vizier's daughter, he'd killed one thousand
women.*

Something went wrong with my efforts. I arrived in the midst of the story and somehow exchanged places with Scheherazade — a phenomena that had never occurred before and that still to this day, I cannot explain.

Now I am trapped in that ancient past. I have taken on Scheherazade's life and the only way I can protect myself and stay alive is to do what she did to protect herself and stay alive.

Every night the King calls for me and listens as I spin tales. And when the evening ends and dawn breaks, I stop at a point that leaves him breathless and yearning for more. And so the King spares my life for one more day, so that he might hear the rest of my dark tale.

As soon as I finish a story... I begin a new one... like the one that you, dear reader, have before you now.

Chapter One

Iron Hall

The last of the preparations had been made for the journey, and Alasdair was ready to set off—more than ready, actually. He wasn't the only one, though. There were dangers, but there always were. He understood them. As a Dragon King, facing threats was just a part of life. Always had been. Even on Earth.

Zora might be a near replica of his home world, but it was also different in many ways. Not to mention the enemies around every corner. Not much worried him, but he would freely admit to being apprehensive about their upcoming expedition. Not for him, though. Nay, his concern was for his mate, Lotti.

Just the thought of her had a flush of desire and love surging through him. Not for the first time, Alasdair wondered if they should have taken this mission. Then again, he and Lotti had set things in motion. They would be the ones to clean things up. Yet a niggle of unease had plagued him for the past few days. One that grew with each passing hour.

Alasdair knew better than to suggest that Lotti remain behind. Just as he would balk if she proposed that to him. Lotti wasn't just any woman. She was special in so many ways. She was one of the Star People, an immortal race of beings who dominated the universe and once held dragons as slaves. Which meant she was more powerful than even a Dragon King. But Lotti had only recently learned who she was and about her powers.

His boots thumped on the stones as he made his way through Iron Hall's vast corridors. The hidden underground city was massive. It had been abandoned many years before, and as a result, some of the hallways had caved in. It now had occupants again. They uncovered more secrets every day while also slowly bringing Iron Hall back to life. What they didn't know, is what happened to the former inhabitants. And they may never uncover that.

The sound of children's laughter reached him as they ran through the corridors, playing. It brought a grin to Alasdair's lips. He was amazed at the bairns' resilience after what they had endured at the hands of those at Stonemore, intent on taking their lives simply because they had been born with magic.

At the thought of the mountainside metropolis, a flood of anger pooled in Alasdair's gut. The source of most of the evil that spread over the land had begun at Stonemore. Iron Hall was the closest city. It also sat halfway beneath the dragon land border, which gave them a slim advantage.

He didn't want to think about the dragons. His kin. Descendants of those from Earth. The same dragons who hated every Dragon King. Not that he blamed them. They had a reason. The Kings had sent the clans away. It didn't matter that they had done it to save the dragons from humans. All those on Zora knew was that they had lost their home to the very species that showed up on their new realm. The Kings wouldn't let the same things that happened on Earth affect Zora.

Alasdair shook off the thoughts that threatened to drag him into melancholy and lengthened his strides. He turned the corner to his and Lotti's chamber to look for his mate. He scanned the room, but there was no sign of her. Alasdair turned on his heel and headed to the main area of Iron Hall. It took him some time. Lotti had wanted a chamber far from the others. Even though she had gained control of her magic, years of unintentionally hurting others was ingrained too deeply. It would take time, and him absorbing her magic if it ever got loose, before she realized she wouldn't harm anyone again.

He picked up voices as he drew near the common area. Alasdair descended a flight of stairs and glanced toward the center where a large pool of water stood. Above it was a huge knot of roots that spread across the open ceiling from a massive tree that hung suspended. Liquid dripped from them into the pool while sunlight filtered through the tangled mass.

"Here he is," Varek said.

Alasdair nodded in greeting and made his way to the trio in the room. Varek ran a hand through his blond hair to shove it away from his face as he said something to his mate, Jeyra. Cullen's mate, Tamlyn, was on Jeyra's other side, her hazel eyes crinkling at the corners as she chuckled.

"I'm looking for Lotti," Alasdair said when he walked up.

"She wanted a quick training session before you left," Tamlyn said before glancing over her shoulder as Sian attempted to corral the children. "I need to help get the kids together. The mission will succeed. I know it."

Alasdair watched her rush to Sian. Tamlyn was a Banshee who saw the tragic deaths of children with magic. She, an Amazon named Jenefer, and Sian, an Alchemist, had worked to save the children. They had been fairly successful even before Cullen joined their undertaking, bringing the Dragon Kings' attention to the problem and thus rescuing even more kids.

Sian shook her wavy brunette locks from her face before putting her fingers to her lips and whistling shrilly. Alasdair winced at the high-pitched sound. The last of the children came running in response. Before Sian followed them, she waved at Alasdair and then cast a look toward the main entrance—something she had done ever since Jenefer left to search for her fellow Amazons to join the fight against Stonemore.

"Are we ready?"

At the sound of Jeyra's question, Alasdair turned to the redhead. Her amber eyes were locked on him. She was a warrior of Orgate, and at one time, Varek's jailer. Varek had been pulled to Zora from Earth by a crone and captured by Jeyra so she could get justice for her family and other Orgateans. Instead, the two uncovered a nest of lies and deceit that rocked the land. They also fell in love.

When Jeyra sided with Varek, her people banished her. Yet she still wore a thick, silver armband on each arm that indicated she hailed from Orgate. And there was a new addition to her left shoulder. A dragon eye tattoo in the same black and red mix of ink as the tattoos on each King that signaled her as a Dragon King's mate.

Alasdair's gaze slid to Varek. His friend watched him carefully with deep brown eyes. He and Varek, like all the Kings, had seen too many villains and wars, but something about Zora was different. The more they dug into its people and history, the more evil was uncovered, and questions arose.

And the more enemies came out of the woodwork.

"You ready, brother?" Varek asked when Alasdair didn't respond.

"Aye. The sooner we get the massirine stone, the better." Anger churned each time Alasdair thought about Villette's people and how they used the stone to spy on the dragons and learn of their movements and locations.

Jeyra nodded as she looked between the two. "Then let's collect Lotti and head out. The sooner we leave, the sooner we can return."

Alasdair agreed. The sound of a crying baby made him pause. It was the bairn who had brought him and Lotti together. Alasdair had already said his farewells to wee Benneit, so there was no reason to delay. Why, then, did he linger?

"What is it?" Varek asked. "Surely, you're no' worried about Lotti. She has more power than we do."

He was worried. His mate might have finally discovered her origins, but there was still so much Lotti didn't know about her abilities or limits. The Star People had once enslaved the dragons. One might have eventually freed them, creating Earth as a refuge—and a hiding place—from the others, but the Star People had found Zora, using it as their playground. They interfered at will, fashioning their own rules as they went. And one of them ruled Stonemore.

Villette. Alasdair clenched his hands into fists. He despised her with every fiber of his being. She was known as the Divine to those who called Stonemore home, using fear and mystery to keep everyone in check. He could lay many crimes at Villette's feet, including the sacrifice of children with magic. But she also held one of theirs—Merrill.

Yet it was another Star Person, Eurielle, who had helped him and Lotti. Despite that, Alasdair didn't trust her. She had let Lotti suffer for years without helping. There was no excuse for that.

"Alasdair?"

He shook himself at Varek's deep frown. "Your mate's correct. There's a lot going on. The Star People, Villette, Merrill still at Stonemore—"

"No' for long," Varek interrupted. "We'll set him free."

"There's also the invisible foe that has it out for us. And let's no' forget the elves. They want a piece of us now, too. Zora was supposed to be a place of peace for the dragons. Maybe they're right. Maybe we brought this. They were fine until we came."

Varek snorted. "They were far from fine, and you know it. They're frightened, and they use us as a place to lay the blame. We're going to sort things out. We'll bring peace once more. But first, we have to find the stone and make sure Villette can no' use it again."

"I know."

Alasdair and Lotti had gotten the stone away from Villette and her people so they could no longer spy on the dragons. The problem was, only a certain group of people on the realm could touch it without the stone killing them. Luckily, Jeyra was one of those people. They guessed it had something to do with those with red hair living longer than other mortals on Zora.

"Then let's go stick one to Villette," Varek said, slapping Alasdair on the arm.

He took one last look around the city before following Varek up the steps to the doorway and then heading outside into the lush canyon. There was a hint of fall in the morning air. The sky was clear, and the canyon teemed with life. Alasdair stopped and raised his gaze to the lip of the canyon. He stood at its narrowest point and spotted Jeyra on the left, climbing her way to the top. Varek jogged in her direction and was beside her in two jumps. Alasdair's gaze swung to the right, and he saw Lotti's wavy, blond hair that just barely touched her shoulders. She had her back to him as she moved her arms. Ever since she'd learned she was a Star Person, she had been pushing herself to learn more about her magic.

For over two hundred years, she had denied her power, fearing it. Alasdair had been the one to convince her to embrace it. She had, yet there was so much for her to learn. He feared there wouldn't be enough time before the brewing war was upon them.

Alasdair heard a chuckle from his other side. He looked over and found Cullen with his legs dangling over the canyon's side. Beside him was none other than the wildcat, Nari. It was as big as a lion with black spotted fur and intelligent green eyes. This particular wildcat had saved Cullen, Shaw, and Lotti from their invisible enemy.

Nari hung around the canyon and could often be found with Cullen. There was a shared fondness between them, given how the cat lay beside Cullen with her large head on his lap as he ran his hand over her thick fur. Alasdair glanced at Varek and Jeyra to see they had reached the top. In two leaps, he was next to Cullen on his other side.

Nari shifted her head and pinned him with her bright green eyes before lazily yawning and stretching out her massive paws, extending her very long, *very* sharp claws for a heartbeat.

"She likes you," Cullen said as he scratched under Nari's chin.

Alasdair didn't answer because his gaze had landed on his mate. The morning sun made her hair appear almost golden as she turned first one way and then the other. He ran his eyes down her body. She had rolled up the sleeves of her light brown undershirt to her elbows and replaced her linen overtunic with a leather corset that conformed to her curves like a second skin. Deep brown breeches hugged her arse and legs before disappearing into knee-high leather boots. She didn't carry a weapon because she *was* a weapon. Lotti hadn't slept much the past few nights. She believed she had something to prove to him and his brethren and had yet to listen, no matter how many times they told her she didn't.

"Are you afraid Lotti can no' handle herself?" Cullen asked.

Alasdair frowned and looked down at him. "She saved my arse at Stonemore."

"Do you no' think you and Varek are up to this task?"

Alasdair rolled his eyes and grunted.

"Then you must be concerned about Jeyra."

Alasdair squatted next to Cullen, knowing what he was doing. "You know I'm no'."

"Yet you're worried, brother."

"We've always been the strongest, the ones with the most power."

"On Earth."

"Aye. My point. This isna our realm."

Cullen nodded and smoothed a hand over Nari's huge head. "And you've found your mate. It's always that way for a King. We never had to worry about losing anything once we sent the dragons away. Our family, our friends…they were gone. Finding love shows us so much, but it also makes us verra aware of what we could lose. Especially those who have no' undergone the mating ceremony."

A ritual that bound the two together so the mate would live as long as the Dragon King. It wasn't exactly immortality, but it was close since it was damned hard to kill a King. Or it had been. He didn't know if the Star People could kill them. He dreaded the idea that they just might be able to.

"At least your mate is protected," Cullen continued. "She is probably more difficult to slay than we are."

Tamlyn bore the dragon eye mark on her left shoulder that pronounced her as Cullen's mate. Alasdair rested a hand on the King's shoulder.

Cullen flashed him a smile and seemed to shove aside his worries. "My point, brother, is that everything will go fine. You and Lotti got the stone away from Villette, and you'll soon discover where you tossed it. Jeyra can retrieve it from the lake. Then, when you four return here, we'll have the stone. And no one can spy on the dragons again."

Alasdair didn't mention that getting back with the stone would be the most dangerous—and difficult—part. And they all knew it. He returned his gaze to Lotti. She faced him now, a smile curving her lips as she watched him with her turquoise eyes. He would never tire of looking at her heart-shaped face or delicate features. Her wide, expressive eyes. Her full lips that could have him on his knees in an instant.

She started walking to the end of the canyon and to him. He straightened, his heart skipping a beat as it always did when she was near. Cullen gave Nari one last pat before climbing to his feet. By the time Lotti reached them, Varek and Jeyra had arrived, as well. Nari hadn't moved from her spot and idly waved the end of her tail.

Alasdair released a long breath. "It's time."

"We'll be here if you need anything," Cullen said.

Varek grinned, a twinkle in his brown eyes. "You're just trying to figure out how to join us."

"I am," Cullen agreed with a wide smile.

They laughed, but it died quickly.

Cullen's pale brown eyes met Alasdair's. "Be safe and hurry back. All of you."

"We will," Lotti replied.

Alasdair took the lead as their journey began. Varek joined him a short while later with Lotti and Jeyra ten steps behind, deep in conversation. Alasdair glanced at Varek to see his gaze turned toward Stonemore. They couldn't see the mountain city lurking like a malevolent soul through the forest that separated them, but everyone knew it was there.

And so was Merrill.

"We'll get him soon," Alasdair vowed.

Varek looked ahead, a muscle ticking in his jaw. "All these weeks of no communication, and when you did get a chance to talk to him, he wouldna leave that hellhole. He stayed."

"To help us."

"Alone. Disconnected from his family. That could put him in a dark place."

Alasdair scoffed. "Merrill? He's the one who always lifts everyone else up. It will take a lot to pull him down."

"I said the same thing. But Jeyra told me something that hasna left me since."

"What's that?"

"She said it's usually the jovial ones like Merrill who have the darkest parts of themselves locked away."

Alasdair glanced at Varek. "You were closest to him. Is that true? Does he have something buried?"

"We all have something buried."

"That's true, but you didna answer my question."

Varek blew out a breath. "Merrill was despondent when we sent our dragons away after the war with the humans. He went to a place I'd never seen before. I couldna reach him, Alasdair. I thought...I thought he was past help. I wanted to do something, but we were all dealing with the loss of our families, friends, and clans. Weeks went by before he reached out."

He paused and audibly swallowed. "I was the one who sank to that awful place. Merrill pulled me out of my despair. I wouldna be here if it were no' for him."

"He did the same for me."

"He did it for *all* of us."

Alasdair winced as the truth dawned on him. "He helped everyone but himself. He buried it."

"Aye. I think he did. And if that gets released while he's trapped in Stonemore, alone with Villette…"

Varek didn't finish. He didn't need to. Alasdair knew exactly what might happen to their brother.

Chapter Two

They covered ground quickly. Lotti had been more than ready to set out on this mission, but now that Iron Hall was behind her, she wanted to turn around and return to the safety of its walls. In all her years, she had never had a home. Somehow, when she least expected it, she had found that at a hidden city. Her gaze locked on Alasdair ahead of her. His shoulder-length auburn hair was loose, except for the top portion he had tied at the back of his head.

She had found more than a place to call home. She had found love. A man who believed in and encouraged her. She'd also found friends. A family. It was more than she ever could've hoped for. And she was terrified of losing it.

As if sensing her gaze, Alasdair glanced over his shoulder at her. Her stomach quivered at his crooked smile and his sherry-colored eyes that matched his hair. Tall and broad-shouldered, he had a face of pleasing angles from his firm jaw to his striking cheekbones and the cleft in his chin. The man was sinfully handsome. She had fallen hard for him once she allowed herself to give in to their attraction.

Through all the hardships they'd endured during their journey to Stonemore, and then within the mountain, his support had never wavered. He had been a steady presence, even when she was overwhelmed. And he was the reason she accepted her magic. He'd risked his life for her, and she hadn't hesitated to do the same for him.

Alasdair showed her what it meant to be a friend. He had a protective nature, and though he struggled to sit by and let her make mistakes at times, he did just that. Because the only way she would learn was by trial and error.

Yet no one was more aware than her that she had only scratched the surface of her abilities. Heading out to retrieve the massirine stone was a huge risk. For one, it killed people who touched it. Or rather, most people. It wouldn't kill a Star Person, but it would render their powers useless for a time. There was also the fact that Villette would be looking for them. Still, it was a risk she and the others had to take to stop the impending war and thwart Villette's plans to destroy all dragons.

Her people had enslaved the dragons long, long ago. And it was one of her people wreaking havoc on Zora now. Villette needed to be stopped, and Lotti intended to do whatever it took to achieve that.

Alasdair said something to Varek before he turned and walked back to her. Jeyra nudged her with an elbow, flashing a knowing smile before jogging to Varek. Lotti's body heated when Alasdair's gaze moved over her.

"It's been quiet," he said, falling into step with her.

She nodded. "I'm not complaining. Let's take it while we can."

"I expected to encounter Stonemore's soldiers by now."

"No doubt we will. Villette probably wants us to believe they're not waiting for us." She thought back to the last time she and Alasdair had faced off against a squad. He had knocked all of them out cold with little effort after absorbing Lotti's magic. "They'll be prepared for us now."

Alasdair's lips flattened. "Aye. Villette will see to that." He made a sound in the back of his throat. "We all assumed the Divine was male."

"To be fair, Villette made sure no one knew she was the Divine. She kept her identity a secret, which only made the mystery that much greater."

Alasdair reached for her hand and linked their fingers. "She's no' done with us. She'll be there."

"And we'll be ready."

He grunted in response.

Lotti knew his thoughts had shifted to his brother, Gordon. Alasdair and the other Kings had racked their brains trying to figure out how Villette had somehow brought Gordon, who had died before the dragons' war with the humans on Earth, back to life. Alasdair had told her the story of how the magic of his realm chose him to be the King of Amethysts, a position previously held by his brother.

Only a Dragon King can kill another King. Gordon no longer served the clan, and the magic knew it wanted him replaced. Alasdair had no choice but to fight his brother to the death to become King.

Then Alasdair had to face Gordon again, but he kept telling Lotti it wasn't his brother. It was Gordon's body, but there was nothing inside. That battle—and the aftermath—still bothered Alasdair. He might have won, but Gordon—or at least his dragon body—was still very much alive.

Villette would no doubt use him again. Alasdair was preparing for that inevitability. He trained relentlessly. The few times he allowed himself to sleep, nightmares of the battle plagued him. Lotti squeezed his hand, wishing she could help. But they each had to sort through their issues to come out victorious.

He glanced at her and smiled. "Lass, you must stop worrying about me."

"I'd suggest the same, but I know it will fall on deaf ears."

His grin widened. "Och. It would."

They paused for a brief rest and lunch and then continued on. A chill raced down Lotti's spine when she recognized the clearing where she had come across Benneit and first met Alasdair. That moment had changed her entire life. She blinked and forced herself away from thoughts of Ben to focus on the present. They had decided to take the long way around the Tunris Mountains while heading west. It added an extra day of travel, but it kept them away from Villette.

Lotti wasn't worried about getting to the lake. Though the problem was, they weren't sure which one Alasdair had propelled the stone to. There were two near the mountains, and they would have to explore each one. The problem was, the longer they were near Stonemore, the greater their chances of encountering the soldiers or Villette.

Villette was furious that Lotti and Alasdair had stolen the stone and slipped from her grasp. She wanted retaliation. Villette would have planned her reckoning down to the last soldier. And when it came, it would be swift and vicious. Villette would wait until they had the stone, then sweep in to take it before turning her attention to the four of them. They were prepared for all of it.

But no one could ever really plan for such things. They came up with scenarios and reactions, and that was all they really could do. Lotti would never forget her first battle with Villette. If Eurielle hadn't interfered, Lotti wasn't sure she would still be standing. She wanted to think she could count on Eurielle in a pinch, but that likely wouldn't happen. If they were to succeed, then Lotti had to anticipate the unforeseen.

There was little talk as they walked. Varek and Jeyra asked questions about the area, and Lotti filled them in on the things she knew from the weather during the seasons, the kind of animals that called it home, and the locations of now-dead cities. There was much of Zora the Dragon Kings hadn't explored yet. Even Jeyra had traveled little outside Orgate before meeting Varek. That meant Lotti was their guide. She pointed out areas she thought might be important either for shelter, food, or defense while the other three would indicate regions good for attack.

The farther they got from Iron Hall, the more restless they became. No one let their guard down. They kept their gazes moving at all times. Only once had they chanced upon someone, and they quickly hid as the travelers moved past them.

Occasionally, Alasdair or Varek broke off to scout ahead or on either side of them, looking for signs that there were soldiers about. Though no one mentioned it, she wondered about the invisible foe and if it would come after them. She hadn't seen it, but she *had* felt it, and she had no desire to run into that thing again. But it was out there. She knew Varek and Alasdair were searching for it, too.

Lotti lay on the blanket and looked up at the stars through the trees when they stopped for the night. It was a stunning evening, but she missed her soft bed. It hadn't taken her long to become accustomed to such a luxury. More than that, she missed Alasdair's hard body beside her. While she and Jeyra needed to sleep, the Kings didn't. Varek stayed in camp to keep watch, while Alasdair went off to do the same from a distance.

Lotti closed her eyes and cleared her mind to find rest. The sounds of the night lulled her, letting her quickly fall asleep. She had barely closed her eyes before someone yanked her up, tightening a hand around her neck that bit into her skin. She gasped in shock as she stared into Villette's face, one side burned, the other beautiful—and filled with disgust and animosity.

"You think you're a champion? A being of good? You think to judge me and your kin for our actions?" she demanded before leaning close, her blue eyes hard and unyielding. "You might want to learn what the significance of your birth is, Destroyer."

Lotti frowned because the words were ones Villette had already said. Lotti struggled against her hold, but she couldn't get free. She turned to her magic, but it didn't answer her. Her heart thudded. This was what she feared. She tried again and again to use her power but it was no use. Villette's hold was too strong.

"Aye. Destroyer. That's what you are," Villette sneered. "The entire universe is at stake as long as you live. It's why you must die."

Villette smiled and released her hold.

Lotti felt air whoosh around her. She tried to think of solid ground to land somewhere unhurt, but she kept falling. Once again, her magic failed her. She screamed for Alasdair, but she was utterly alone except for Villette's laughter ringing loudly around her. Lotti looked down to see the ground rising quickly. She was plummeting to her death.

Suddenly, Lotti's eyes opened, and she bolted upright, gasping for breath.

"Hey. Lotti, love. Look at me."

Large, strong hands gently framed her face. She turned toward the sound of Alasdair's deep, soothing, accented voice and stared into his eyes.

His gaze searched hers before a small frown furrowed his brow. "It was a dream. You're all right."

She squeezed her eyes closed and threw her arms around his neck. He didn't release her until she stopped shaking. She leaned back to see the first streaks of light in the sky. Dawn had arrived.

"Want to talk about it?" Alasdair asked as he handed her a waterskin.

She drank her fill and wiped her mouth with the back of her hand before telling him about the nightmare. "What if she's right? What if I'm responsible for everyone's death? What if I do destroy everything? I've hurt people before."

"Only because you fought against your magic and lost control. I doona believe Villette. She's bitter and full of rage. She will say anything to get a jab in at someone. If there is a Destroyer, it isna you. Someone with as much love to give as you have, can no' be the one meant to wipe out existence."

"But what *if?*"

Alasdair tucked a strand of her hair behind her ear. "You're a good person. You've never intentionally hurt anyone who wasna trying to harm you. If you were the Destroyer, then that wouldna apply to you."

She wasn't so sure of that. "I couldn't use my magic."

"You've told me before that your greatest fear isna being able to use it. Dreams have a way of taking our worries and fears and compounding them by a million. Then there's the fact that you've had a difficult time sleeping the past few nights. Exhaustion finally caught up."

"Maybe. Probably," she added with a sigh.

"Since you learned about your powers, have they failed you?"

"Well…nay," she admitted.

"Then there's no reason to think they will when you need them."

Lotti wanted to believe him. Alasdair's words were wise, but she couldn't entirely stamp out the doubt. She glanced around their camp, noticing for the first time that Varek and Jeyra weren't there.

"They gave us some privacy," Alasdair said.

Lotti pulled her knees up so her feet rested on the ground. The longer she was awake, the less of a hold the nightmare had on her.

Alasdair glanced into the woods. "You know verra little about your people. You can no' trust Villette, and Eurielle didna share much."

"She will. She promised. I do wish I had someone to talk to about all of this."

"You might."

She nodded as she drank more water. "You're talking about Erith?"

"She created this realm for the dragons. Rhi went to warn her about the Star People, and Erith isna one to run from a fight. She'll come. If for no other reason than to get answers for herself. She's a friend and willna stand with Villette and those swayed by her."

"You can't know that."

He gave her a crooked grin. "Aye, lass. I do know that." He ran his finger along her jaw. "You got free of Villette once. You know who you are now, and you're learning your powers. Whatever advantage she had is gone. You doona need to fear her. Doona underestimate her, but doona fear her."

Lotti was the only one who could fight against the Star People. The more she gave in to panic, the more Villette won. "Good advice."

Alasdair got to his feet and held out his hand to pull her up. "Ready?"

"Ready," she said, dusting off her bum before catching a biscuit he tossed her way.

Chapter Three

It was quiet. Too quiet. Alasdair hadn't spent much time on Zora, but his senses were telling him something was wrong. He glanced at Varek to see his friend's lips compressed and his gaze searching. A glance confirmed that Lotti and Jeyra were also on edge.

Varek looked his way and motioned with his head that he would move forward. Alasdair nodded and slowed his steps to put the women between them. Neither of them were defenseless. Lotti had her magic, and Jeyra was a skilled warrior. But neither Jeyra nor Varek had gone up against the Star People. They were unpredictable and volatile.

It would be easier if he and Varek could shift into their true forms. They could fly to the lakes in short order instead of walking, but the realm was on the brink of war, and flying could be the match that started it all. It didn't help that Villette had stirred the humans, getting them to despise the dragons. It didn't matter that a barrier had been erected to keep mortals out of dragon country. Somehow, the old hatred from Earth had spilled over onto Zora.

This realm was meant to be a place of peace for the dragons after they lost everything. And yet, generations later, they were about to experience the same struggle their ancestors did. It infuriated Alasdair. Each King had sacrificed everything they had to keep their dragons safe. Many of them—him included—had nearly succumbed to grief and depression in the wake of the dragons' departure.

Alasdair had slept for centuries just to shut out the mortals as they continued living as if nothing had happened. When Alasdair woke, he found that humans had changed very little. There were many advancements, but the race was still as covetous and egocentric as ever.

The Kings rejoiced when they finally found the dragons. For a short time, the weight of regret and guilt that Alasdair had carried fell away. Then the Kings learned something hunted the dragons. None of them had hesitated to cross the realms to fight for their brethren. Only the dragons didn't want the Kings.

Where the dragons had once belonged to clans each ruled by a King, that structure was no more on this new realm. They intermingled as one clan. It was a beautiful sight to behold. While Erith had created Zora in Earth's image, the realm didn't have the same magic as home. Kings were chosen by the magic on Earth. Without it, the clans were no more. And with that gone, there was no need for the Kings.

Yet the dragons weren't alone. They had Brandr and Eurwen. The twins weren't just any children. They were the offspring of Constantine, King of Dragon Kings, and Rhi, a powerful Light Fae. Brandr and Eurwen had done a good job of ruling the dragons, but nothing could quell the lingering anger directed at every Dragon King for not eradicating the mortals on Earth to end the war—humans who had somehow found a way to Zora.

Alasdair had stayed true to himself, the magic that had chosen him, and the vow he and every King had made to protect the mortals when they arrived on Earth. No matter how hard he tried, he couldn't pinpoint when things had gone wrong. And there was no use attempting that on Zora.

The dragons hated the Kings nearly as much as they abhorred the mortals. They only tolerated the Kings because they were fighting the battles to keep the dragons out of it this time. Alasdair prayed it worked. Maybe it would make up for the past. Perhaps it would rid the dragons of some of their animosity.

Varek halted and raised a hand. Jeyra immediately squatted, and Lotti followed suit. Alasdair turned his head slightly and looked to the side. He shifted sideways to keep an eye on the others and look behind him. No movement suggested someone was following them, but that didn't mean one of the Star People wasn't there. He didn't know if they could hide themselves. Actually, there wasn't much they *did* know about the race, only that they were formidable.

Alasdair turned when he heard Varek swear. He followed his friend's gaze up into a tree and saw the end of a long, black tail.

"It's a wildcat," Varek said.

Alasdair took one more look behind him before striding to Lotti and Jeyra. He touched Lotti's arm before swinging his gaze to Varek. "We need to pick up the pace."

"Good," Jeyra said. "I don't like it here."

Varek flexed his hands. "None of us does. Point us in the right direction, Lotti, and we'll get moving."

"Keep going west for now. We need to get past the mountains before we head north," she said.

The mountains rose behind Lotti like stone giants. They had nearly been trapped there. He'd rather not see that place again, but he knew without a doubt they would return to the mountains and Stonemore soon.

"I'm going ahead," Varek told them.

Alasdair nodded his agreement. Jeyra and Varek shared a look before he turned on his heel and jogged away.

"I'll take the rear," Alasdair told the girls.

Lotti glanced at the Tunris Mountains behind her before walking past Jeyra. "Follow me."

Lotti kept up a quick and steady pace, deftly steering them through forests and clearings. They had been traveling for an hour when Varek suddenly appeared. Alasdair heard the clink of armor as Varek motioned them to his right toward a cluster of dense brush. Alasdair and the girls ran toward it, hunkering down moments before a group of Stonemore soldiers appeared.

"They're looking for someone," Varek whispered beside them.

Lotti's lips twisted. "Us, you mean."

"Most likely," Alasdair agreed.

Jeyra watched the soldiers through the foliage. "Stupid of them to travel like that. Anyone could hear them. They should fan out and move more stealthily."

"Aye. I didna think they were that stupid," Varek added.

Alasdair glanced to the side and met Lotti's gaze. "They're no'. This is a diversion." He sat back on his haunches and waited until the last of the soldiers were past them before meeting the others' gazes. "Villette would never send out a troop like that. As you said, Jeyra, they make too much noise."

"Bloody hell," Varek said as he braced a fist on the ground. "Villette thinks to trap us."

Lotti shifted to lean back against a tree. "She wants to prove she's smarter than everyone."

"She has no idea where the stone is. How does she know where to station soldiers?" Jeyra asked.

Alasdair looked through the branches to the mountain. "She's guessing. The stone is gone, and she knows Lotti and I had something to do with it."

"She's no' following us," Varek said.

Alasdair shook his head. "No one is."

"Unless she doesn't have to," Lotti said into the silence that followed. "What if she knows where I am?"

Alasdair thought about that for a second before saying, "I doona think she does. She didna know where Eurielle was. Villette had no idea where you were all those years, and I think that still holds. Can you tell where she is? Where any of your people are?"

"Nay, but what if that's only because I don't know how."

Varek shrugged a shoulder. "I agree. If Villette could find you, she would've done it over the last few days and attempted to force you to tell her where the stone is."

"Maybe," Lotti said. "But that doesn't tell us how she knew where we're going."

Jeyra wrinkled her nose. "I hate to say it, but maybe she is smart enough to deduce where the stone could be. Perhaps she figured that out and is waiting to see who comes for it and when."

"Shite," Varek murmured.

It had been wishful thinking that they could sneak to the lakes to search without being noticed. They had all expected something like this. It didn't make it any easier to swallow, however.

"Not a problem. We find those stationed to watch and take them out," Jeyra stated.

Lotti picked up a fallen leaf and twirled the stem between her fingers. "That won't work. The instant they don't check in, Villette will know."

"If we doona do something, they'll alert her and come after us," Varek pointed out.

Alasdair grinned as he looked at each of them. "Unless we create a diversion of our own."

"We'll only have one chance at it," Lotti said.

Varek shrugged. "We'll make it work."

"First, we need to know which lake." Jeyra pinned her gaze on him.

Alasdair blew out a breath. "When I hurled the stone through the mountain with my magic, I thought of the closest lake."

"There are two," Varek said.

Alasdair cut his gaze to him. "I'm aware."

"Villette may have people watching the lakes," Lotti added.

Jeyra sat cross-legged on the ground. "We should assume she does."

"Let's just presume they're watching the entire area," Varek said.

Alasdair hated to admit he was probably right. "The way has been clear so far, but we should proceed as if it hasna. Villette doesna know what you look like, Jeyra. You should get past them easily." He looked from Lotti to Varek. "No' so for the rest of us. She somehow knows the Dragon Kings."

"Which means she'll know me," Varek said with a nod. "But Jeyra can no' go on her own. I need to be with her to help her reach the stone at the bottom of the lake."

Lotti suddenly grinned. "Not if you and Alasdair are the distraction."

"I like the way you think," Jeyra told her with a smile.

Alasdair narrowed his eyes. "What are you thinking?"

"You two are dragons." Lotti shrugged. "We use that."

Varek pulled a face. "We're trying to prevent a war. Humans tend to freak out when they see us in our true forms."

"No' all of them." Alasdair smiled as he realized what Lotti was getting at. "Villette is using my brother's body. Those within the mountain who work for her know all about dragons. They're no' as frightened as others."

Varek's face went slack as he pieced things together. "Ah. I see. Alasdair, you draw them out, and I'll use my power to incapacitate them."

Lotti raised her brows and nodded. "The moment Villette realizes her people have been disabled, she'll come at us with everything she has."

"What's the quickest way back to Iron Hall?" Jeyra asked.

Varek's face folded into a grimace. "Please doona say through the mountain."

"Through the mountain," Lotti answered.

Jeyra met Lotti's gaze and shrugged. "She'd never expect us to do that."

"That's insane. You two barely got out the first time," Varek stated irritably as he looked between Alasdair and Lotti.

Alasdair ran a hand over his jaw. "We were no' going through then. I was looking for Merrill. That's different."

"She'll likely have reinforced every entrance and exit," Lotti added.

Varek shook his head. "We're no' going into that fucking mountain."

"Then what do you suggest?" Jeyra asked.

Varek grinned. "We do the verra thing we're no' supposed to do. We fly back. Lotti can make us invisible so no one sees."

"That could work," Lotti said.

Alasdair knew it was probably their best option. But it wouldn't be as easy as all that. Villette hadn't hesitated to use Gordon. She would again. And if she had Gordon, what other dead dragon's body did she have? "That's only if we doona have any other options."

"We could split up," Jeyra suggested.

Varek firmly shook his head. "Absolutely, no'. They'll know you have the stone, and they'll make a beeline for you."

"He's right," Lotti said. "We have to stick together when we leave. I also agree with Alasdair. We get as far as we can on our own."

"Then we fly," Alasdair said.

Chapter Four

Lotti had spent the majority of her life avoiding people at all costs. But it was different when she could take her time to pick her way through the country. That wasn't the case now.

They had opted to give the mountains an even wider berth than she'd originally set, but that also allowed them to continue moving at a decent clip. Alasdair took the lead, scouting far ahead. He used his mental link with Varek to notify them that he had located individuals set high in the trees, watching for them. They could then bypass those scouts.

Jeyra was the one without magic, but Lotti felt out of place. She knew little about battle. She had held her own when she faced Villette and the soldiers inside the mountain, but this was different. She could feel it in her bones. Too much rested on them obtaining the stone.

And Villette wanted it back.

Lotti tried not to think about her nemesis, but it was nearly impossible. Everything she and the others had done was because of Villette and the Star People. *Her* people. Lotti didn't want to be a Star Person. She was mortified to know what type of beings they were. But she couldn't change her origins. The only things she could control were her decisions, actions, and words.

The Star People might believe she was the Destroyer, but that could mean anything. For all she knew, it meant she had been born to destroy *them*. No one knew. Or if they did, they weren't sharing it with her. Alasdair was right. She had the capacity to decide what she was to become. And right now, she was fighting for the dragons and everyone with them. She had chosen a side. No one wanted a war, but wishing alone wouldn't stop one from starting. It took action. Like what they were doing now.

Varek pushed them hard. There was no conversing as they quietly moved over the land. Just after midday, they stopped long enough for her and Jeyra to rest and eat. Then they were on their feet again. This time, Varek scouted ahead, and Alasdair stayed with them.

Lotti wiped the sweat from her brow on her shirt sleeve. She was tired, but there was no use complaining when they had more ground to cover. A half an hour later, she felt Alasdair move up beside her.

"How are you doing?" he asked.

She gave him a quick smile. "I'm fine. Have you remembered anything about the lake?"

"I didna see it when I sent the stone to it."

"That will make things difficult."

He grunted softly. "I've been thinking about where we were in the mountain. Imagine us within the mountain, facing out. Now, by my guess, we were toward the right side."

"I believe you're right," she said, pulling up her memories. "The entry was toward the middle left, but we wove through so many passages I can't be sure."

Alasdair shoved a branch aside so they could walk past. "It's all I've been considering. I know it took us some time to find our way back to the entrance, and we were headed toward the left the entire time."

"Then you're correct. We would've been more toward the right side."

"Does that help in figuring out which lake?"

She nodded, briefly meeting his gaze. "It does."

"Let's hope I'm right."

"You are."

Alasdair's lips curved into a grin.

Lotti pictured their current route in her head and thought about the body of water closest to the far side of the mountain. "We need to go to Narrow Lake. It's a little farther, but that is the one nearest to where we were in the mountain."

"Good."

"Maybe. It also means we need to think about whether we head straight there or circle around."

Jeyra glanced at them over her shoulder. "How much longer will it take to go around?"

"Two days if we go at this speed."

Alasdair was silent for a heartbeat before asking, "How soon if we take a direct route?"

"We could be there by nightfall if we don't run into anyone."

Jeyra shrugged without looking their way. "We'll run into Villette's people sooner or later. The longer we're out here, the more time we give them to figure out what we're doing."

"Hold up," Alasdair told them.

Lotti and Jeyra halted immediately. "What is it?" Lotti asked.

Alasdair faced her but slid a quick look to Jeyra. "I've alerted Varek. He's on his way back." Alasdair then focused on her. "Can you draw the area for me?"

Lotti looked around for some dirt so she could give him what he wanted, but there was too much grass. She gathered some sticks, pinecones, rocks, and anything else she could find before kneeling near some cover and laying everything out. When she finished, Varek had returned.

"Okay," she said as she sat back.

The others lowered themselves to the ground to get a better view of things.

Lotti pointed to an acorn. "This is us." She used a stick to circle an area. "This is the forest, which extends for quite a way north and west."

"Perfect, if we're trying to hide," Jeyra said.

Varek scratched his cheek. "Also great for others to hide in wait for us."

Lotti pointed the stick toward a short stack of small rocks. "Here is the mountain. The range is considerable, but for our purposes, I'm just using the section we were in and where Stonemore is located." She paused before indicating two pinecones. "These are the lakes. By Alasdair's calculations, we need to head to Narrow Lake. Here," she said, motioning to the pinecone farthest from them.

"That's a lot of forest between us and the lake," Jeyra pointed out.

Varek twisted his lips ruefully. "There are no good options here."

"There usually never are," Alasdair replied.

Jeyra looked at Lotti. "You know this land. Should we go all the way around the forest or through?"

"There are risks either way. The longer we leave the stone, the more chance Villette has to locate it." Lotti blew out a breath and sat back. "I think we go through."

Alasdair nodded. "I agree."

"Through it is, then. What's our path?" Varek asked.

Lotti gripped the stick with both hands and held it upright in the ground, resting her chin on her hands. "As straight as we can."

"We'll scout ahead again and use magic to expand that," Alasdair said.

Varek frowned. "Is that wise? We know Villette could sense magic when Merrill and Shaw were in Stonemore. I'm no' sure we should take that chance now."

"I doona think we have a choice. We willna be able to see everyone."

Lotti said, "Don't forget, we have the diversion."

"It'll have to be a big one if we still need to get through the forest to the lake," Jeyra said.

Alasdair tapped a finger on his leg, considering. "It will be."

"Let's just hope I don't choose the wrong body of water," Jeyra added.

Lotti slowly released a breath. "You won't. Because I'll be with you."

"Lotti," Alasdair began.

She quickly cut him off. "I know what you're going to say, but I'm the only one who knows the area and can get Jeyra there. You and Varek cause enough of a distraction that no one notices us."

"I no' thrilled with it," Varek muttered. "But it could work."

Jeyra rested her hand on her mate's arm. "Because it will."

"Alasdair?" Lotti pushed when he said no more.

He shook his head. "I doona like this either, but it's the best option. Varek and I will get to you if anything goes wrong."

"We need to set up a meeting place in case things do go wrong," Jeyra suggested.

Everyone looked at Lotti. She glanced down at her makeshift map and considered all the options. It had to be somewhere that would be easy to get to but also difficult for anyone chasing them. She also had to consider the size in case Alasdair and Varek needed to shift.

Lotti used the stick to indicate the north side of the lake. "There's a cliff here. You can't miss it. It's a sheer climb to the top unless you know the concealed steps. We'll head up if we can. Regardless, we meet there."

"Is there somewhere to hide at the bottom?" Alasdair asked.

She nodded. "Plenty of places."

"You two would be out in the open while going around the lake," Varek pointed out.

Jeyra nudged him with her elbow. "We can do this. Besides, I'm more worried about the lake itself."

"We should've brought more people," he muttered.

Lotti pointed at the acorn. "We'll meet back here if all goes well."

Alasdair looked between her and Jeyra. "If, at any time, things get too dicey, get somewhere safe. I doona care if you have the stone or no'. We'll find you."

"You forget that Varek and I are mated now. My life is tied to his. I only die if he does," Jeyra said.

Varek pulled her to him and gave her a quick kiss. "I'd rather you stay safe."

"If Villette could've killed me, she would've done it already. I'll be fine," Lotti said.

Alasdair squeezed the bridge of his nose between his thumb and forefinger. "Everything can die. There are things on Zora that could affect us differently than in our world. I,"—he paused and glanced at Varek before his gaze slid to Lotti—"*we* doona want to lose *you.*"

"We won't be reckless," Jeyra promised.

Lotti reached for Alasdair and linked her fingers with his. "But we have an important mission that must be completed. We'll be careful. And we ask the same of you."

"We will," Alasdair promised.

Varek nodded. "Aye. We will."

The longer they wasted, the more daylight they lost. Lotti stood and pulled Alasdair up beside her. She flattened her hands on his chest as Varek and Jeyra moved away to speak privately.

"Are you sure about this?" Alasdair asked.

"Do you trust I can get to the lake and find the stone?"

His sherry eyes searched hers. "You know I do."

"Then trust that I'm sure about this plan. I was with you in the mountain. I know exactly what the stone can do in Villette's hands. We will retrieve it and take it far from here so it can't be used against the dragons."

Alasdair grinned, stepped closer, and wound his arms around her. "You're risking a lot for the dragons."

"I'd risk everything for you. And by extension, the dragons *are* you."

"Och, lass, I love you."

She smoothed her hands over his shoulders and around his neck. "I love you."

Their lips met in a soft kiss filled with love and hope. She sank her fingers into his thick hair when he deepened the kiss, sweeping his tongue into her mouth to tangle with hers. His hands splayed on her back, holding her firmly against him.

He gradually ended the kiss and then pressed his forehead to hers. They stood like that, in each other's arms, for a long minute.

"Come back to me," he told her.

Lotti lifted her head to look at him. "Always."

It killed her to step out of his arms, but she did. He lingered until he had to drop her hand. She took a deep breath and then slowly released it. "Be safe."

"Always," he replied with a wink.

Grass crunched beneath her feet as Jeyra walked to her. Lotti looked over and met the warrior's gaze. She took one more look at Alasdair before turning and heading into the forest with Jeyra.

"We've got this," the warrior whispered.

Lotti waited until the trees had enveloped them before saying, "Aye, we do."

Chapter Five

"You good, brother?"

Alasdair had to remind himself he wasn't the only one watching his mate walk straight toward danger. He steeled himself and swung his head to Varek. "I will be when this is over."

"Aye. I feel that." Varek drew in a deep breath and slowly released it. "I doona know about you, but I'm more than ready to cause a ruckus."

"The bigger, the better."

"That could verra well draw out your brother again."

Alasdair glanced toward the mountains. "If that's what it takes to give the lasses time to find the stone and get away, then so be it."

"We willna know where they are or if they're in trouble."

"Lotti will protect them. They need time, and we're going to make sure they have every second."

Varek nodded once. "Shall we begin?"

"I'll go first and draw them out. Stay behind me and out of sight. I doona want anyone seeing you until they're gathered around me. We need as many of them as we can get."

"No' all will come."

"Enough will. Then you can knock everyone unconscious."

A muscle ticked in Varek's jaw. "Gladly."

Alasdair started to turn away but paused and looked at Varek. "If another dragon attacks, doona engage."

"You can no' be serious."

"It'll be up to you to find Lotti and Jeyra and get them across the border to the dragons."

Varek's nostrils flared, his irritation evident. "We've already lost Merrill. I'm no' losing you to Villette."

"If she does take me, it might give me access to Merrill. Regardless, I willna be staying. I'll find a way out."

"You willna have to. I'll be coming for both you *and* Merrill, and I willna be alone. Lotti will be right beside me."

Alasdair faced Varek. "There's no doubt Lotti's power is potent, but I doona want her engaging with Villette or any of the Star People again until she's had more time to understand her magic."

"Then you shouldna have brought her along."

Unfortunately, Varek was right, but there was no use debating that now. "I'm a Dragon King, brother. I can survive whatever Villette throws at me."

"I'm no' questioning your strength or willpower. I'm doubting your decision. Merrill is close but out of reach. We can no' even talk to him. I willna lose another brother to that fucking city. If they capture you, the war that Eurwen and Brandr have staved off will be at our doorstep, and I willna be the only King busting through the gates of Stonemore. So, doona get caught."

Alasdair clamped a hand on Varek's shoulder and squeezed. He knew Varek had struggled with Merrill willingly remaining at Stonemore, but Alasdair hadn't known the depths of it until that moment. He held Varek's gaze. "I willna get caught."

"Thank you." He shook his head. "Now, let's get these bastards."

Alasdair dropped his arm to his side and looked at the thick forest. He hated not being with Lotti, but she knew the woods better than any of them. He trusted her to get herself and Jeyra to the lake. Besides, he felt sorry for anyone who tried to stop either of them. They wouldn't hesitate to strike.

"Doona kill unless you have to," Alasdair said.

Varek grunted. "I'll do my best."

With that, Alasdair strode to the edge of the forest. He slipped between two enormous trees and was instantly enveloped in another world. Sunlight filtered through the dense canopy. Birdsong rang out around him. Wildflowers, plants, moss, and other lichen thrived. Mushrooms dotted the ground and the trees.

He heard the flapping of wings from a bird nearby. There was an unmistakable scraping sound like a squirrel makes when gnawing on a nut. He opened his enhanced hearing to see if he could pick up anything from Lotti and Jeyra. It took a moment, but he heard two people moving through the forest.

Alasdair opened his mental link with Varek and said, *"I hear the girls."*

"Aye. I also picked up a sound ahead to the left, high in the trees. Could be an animal. Or—"

"Could be someone keeping watch."

"I'm fifty paces behind you to the left."

"Stay alert."

Varek snorted. *"I'm no' the one drawing out the enemy."*

Alasdair bit back a smile as Varek severed the link. He stealthily moved through the woods, keeping close to the trees as he scanned the area. He startled a deer off to his right, and it ran away. Alasdair halted and studied the area where the deer had been. Minutes ticked by with nothing before he finally saw movement in the branches. The man wore brown, allowing him to blend into the trunks of the trees. Once Alasdair spotted him, however, he couldn't believe he hadn't seen him before. The question was whether the watcher had spotted *him*.

"Found another. Eight meters to my right. He's on a lower branch, facing away from me and camouflaged in brown," Alasdair told Varek.

There was a moment of silence before Varek said, *"Got him."*

Alasdair wanted to get deeper into the forest before anyone saw him. He glanced at the man in the tree once more before moving on. Alasdair studied the trees more carefully as he picked his way through the trunks and undergrowth. The forest remained quiet as he walked deeper into the region. He considered it a triumph every minute that passed without anyone spotting Lotti and Jeyra.

He knew the time had come to begin the diversion when he caught sight of another guard in a tree, scanning the area where Alasdair was. He hadn't found him yet, but he would as soon as Alasdair moved.

"It's time," Alasdair warned Varek.

"Ready when you are, brother."

Alasdair pulled his gaze away from the guard and walked from behind the tree. He only took two steps before he heard a shout. Within moments, the forest was a flurry of activity, with men descending from trees and rushing toward him while animals bolted away in surprise. He turned in a circle and looked at the faces of those surrounding him. There were only six, but he heard more rushing toward him.

The men had drawn swords, and Alasdair nearly laughed. He could end their lives in a blink. He continued to stare as more men came. Some had fear in their eyes. Others had excitement. They knew the Divine wanted him, but he doubted they knew who he really was. But they were about to.

"The Divine wants you," a deep voice said from behind him.

Alasdair slowly turned around and locked his gaze on an older soldier with gray at the temples of his brown hair and deep grooves on his face from too much time in the sun. There were also visible battle scars on his neck and forearms. "So?"

"You're coming with us."

Alasdair stood calmly, which only agitated those already frightened. "I'm no' going anywhere with you."

"You're surrounded," the older soldier stated, a small frown furrowing his brow. "You don't have a choice."

"There's always a choice. You made the wrong one when you came here to catch me."

The leader narrowed his pale blue eyes, studying Alasdair. "We were told to bring you in, and that's what we're going to do."

"If you knew what I really was, you'd be running for your lives." Alasdair saw a couple of soldiers out of the corner of his eye, exchanging a look and taking a step back. He cut a look at them before sliding his gaze back to the leader. "Doona say I didna warn you."

Alasdair grinned and then shifted. The space was too small. Trees snapped and toppled, their groans drowned out by the soldiers' shouts of fear and shock. Alasdair swiped out with his tail, knocking down men and more trees. He hated causing such damage in the forest, but he needed to be able to move.

Arrows pinged against his scales. Some men grouped together and attempted an attack while others rushed to hide or run away. Alasdair turned and swung his tail again, creating more space. He let out a low growl when a sword flew at his face, coming close to his eye.

"More are coming," Varek warned.

Alasdair flicked his front foot to toss away a soldier attempting to climb him. The man screamed as he flew through the air before hitting a tree and crumpling to the ground. Those who dared to attack him were few, and one of them was the leader. He locked eyes with the older soldier, who shouted orders to the men still standing.

It would be so easy to kill them. Villette knew it was possible, yet she'd sent the squadron out anyway. She wanted war. She had stirred hatred for dragons among the humans. All those stories about dragons leaving their land to terrorize the mortals was true. The only difference was, the dragon was most likely Gordon. If Alasdair killed any soldiers, it would only fan the flames, bringing hostilities that much closer.

He and the other Kings knew full well what such a conflict entailed—both during and after. There were never any winners. There were only lives lost. And all for what? Because someone wanted what someone else had. It was the same vicious cycle all over again.

Alasdair used to have more hope for the universe. He used to believe that humans could be good and kind. Those who didn't believe in taking whatever they wanted. The war on Earth had shattered that belief. It sickened him to know that those like Villette perpetrated the same vitriol and selfishness. But Villette had been stirring up dissent between the mortals and dragons for centuries, swelling the human's hatred to a boiling point.

Nothing the dragons did or didn't do would stop what was coming. He recognized that and suspected many of the other Kings did, too. However, Eurwen and Brandr did not. Not yet. The twins were holding on to hope, just as the Kings once had on Earth. And look how that had turned out. They'd sent the dragons away and gone into hiding while the mortals took over.

That couldn't happen on Zora.

He wouldn't let it.

Chapter Six

Lotti had traversed the forest many times. There were always predators, be they animals or humans. During those years, she had kept to herself. The advantage was that she'd learned to blend in with nature. It had kept her safe many times. But that wasn't helping now.

Not when so much was on the line.

Jeyra walked half a step behind her. The warrior carefully placed each foot as she moved as quietly as Lotti. Both were on alert and hyper-aware of every sound and movement, most of which were nothing more than animals. But then there were the others.

Lotti was the first to spot one of the guards. Dressed in brown from head to toe, he sat in a set of bushes near a cluster of trees, eating. She reached out a hand and tapped Jeyra. The warrior nodded, acknowledging that she had seen the man. They crouched down before carefully moving out of sight.

"That was close," Jeyra whispered when they were clear.

Lotti nodded. "Too close."

"How much farther to the lake?"

"At this rate, we'll be lucky to reach it today."

Jeyra wrinkled her nose in distaste. "We need the boys to start the diversion."

"When they do, we'll have to move fast."

"They'll draw out most of those on watch, but not everyone. We should be prepared for that."

Lotti shoved at the hair sticking to her face. The forest was still and humid. That and the apprehension of their mission caused her to sweat. "Those who hang back will be few. We should be able to dodge or incapacitate them."

"I always like a challenge," Jeyra said with a grin.

Lotti chuckled and shook her head as she looked around them.

"There's a stream near here. It cuts through a sizable hill. The ravine will be good cover, though it's slow-going."

"Whatever prevents us from being found."

"This way," Lotti said and crept from their hiding spot.

She continued for a bit before diverting to the side. A smile split her lips when she crested the chasm and looked down at the water. The stream was shallow and moved slowly, creating an oasis in the middle of the forest. Lotti picked her way down the steep hill, trying not to disturb too much of the ground in case someone followed them.

A large tree had fallen across the stream, though its roots were still in the ground. Moss covered the trunk, the rocks, and every other nearby surface. The ground around the stream was thickly carpeted with plants wherever the large boulders were absent. She and Jeyra kept close to the side of the hill as they climbed over fallen logs, rocks, and massive root balls.

The way was slippery and treacherous, but most of the trees were too young to hold anyone on their limbs and too skinny for anyone to hide behind. But she and Jeyra kept an eye on either side of the gully in case someone was stationed above.

They covered a considerable distance. Lotti felt good about the decision to venture down to the water until she heard a shout. Both she and Jeyra halted and pressed into the side of the ravine as they listened to men calling to each other all around them. She exchanged a worried look with Jeyra.

It felt like an eternity later before the footsteps of the last men faded, presumably heading straight to Alasdair. She knew he could handle himself, he was a powerful Dragon King, but that didn't make her worry any less. How could it when her heart was involved?

Lotti focused on the stream and watched the water flowing tranquilly downhill, weaving over and around rocks and roots. She didn't look up until she heard the crash of falling trees.

"That's our sign," Jeyra said.

They pushed away from the hillside and began moving quickly until they reached another hill where the water spilled from a gap in the rocks midway up to fall over the side and down to the stream below.

Lotti had already turned them to the right and moved toward a slope with a better climbing angle. Her fingers sank into decaying leaves and dirt as she pulled herself up to the top as quickly as possible. There were no sounds of being chased or shouts for them to halt, so they kept going.

Jeyra got to the top first and reached out a hand to help Lotti over.

They took a second to rest and look around.

"You probably could've levitated," Jeyra whispered.

Lotti nodded, knowing she was right. "I'm still getting used to my abilities. Though it would've saved us some time and energy."

"It might have also brought attention to us that we don't need. Ready?"

Lotti pointed forward. "This way. The lake is a straight shot from here."

The ground was fairly even, and they used the advantage to run. Lotti once more led while Jeyra watched their backs. There was no road through the forest, but there were game trails. Lotti used those because they were easier to navigate.

She jerked when she heard a dragon roar, but she didn't slow. It was behind her. Was it Alasdair or Varek? Or was it Gordon? All she could hope for was that Alasdair and Varek were able to get away when it was time.

Something fell in front of Lotti, blocking her path. She drew up with barely enough time to stop herself from running into it. Jeyra let out a curse behind her, and Lotti realized it was a soldier. She didn't hesitate to summon a wave of her magic. It moved like ripples through the air, slamming into him just as he reached for her. He flew back, toppling heels over head.

A groan escaped him, and he slowly rolled to the side to sit up. Jeyra rushed past her and launched herself at the soldier. There was a thud before the man slumped to the ground, unmoving.

Jeyra straightened and flipped her dagger over before sheathing it. "That knock on the head will keep him asleep for some time."

They didn't linger. Lotti ran and didn't stop, not when her lungs burned, not when her side cramped, and not when her legs threatened to give out. They didn't encounter anyone else, but she couldn't shake the feeling that they were rushing toward trouble. However, there wasn't time to consider that—not when time wasn't on their side. They still had to search the lake.

Lotti deviated from the game trail and moved over undulating ground. It slowed them down, but they didn't stop. Not until she saw the lake through a break in the trees. She pulled up just inside the forest.

"I've not heard anything else from the boys," Jeyra said between ragged breaths as she looked behind her.

Lotti found her gaze pulled in the same direction as she braced her hands on her knees and gulped in air. She wished she could talk mentally to Alasdair like the dragons could. She needed to know if he was okay. But if she let herself linger on all the possible ways he could be injured, she would never do anything else. She had to push those thoughts aside and concentrate on the matter at hand.

"I'm a decent swimmer, but not good enough to swim that."

Lotti straightened and looked at the lake with Jeyra. She swallowed, her mouth dry. Somehow, Jeyra had regained her breath while Lotti was still trying to slow hers. "I'll bet Alasdair put the stone in the deepest part."

"And how deep is the lake?"

Lotti heard the concern in Jeyra's voice. She looked at her and decided it was best not to give her that information just yet. "Deep."

"I was afraid you were going to say that. We never discussed how to get the stone. I knew I'd be diving, but..."

"We believed all four of us would be working together."

"Plans changed. As they do," Jeyra said with a shrug.

Lotti nodded and gazed at the brilliant blue water. Sweat dripped into her eye, and she blinked it away. "We've adapted. We will for this new problem, too."

"I wouldn't call this a new problem." Jeyra grinned, attempting to lighten the mood. "Can you swim?"

"Aye, but you have to be the one to touch the stone."

"Because it kills everyone else." Jeyra's lips twisted. "Hurray for me. How are we going to get it?"

Now wasn't the time for Lotti to test her powers. What if something went wrong? But they really had no choice. She seemed to be saying that a lot, which wasn't a good sign. Ever.

"You have an idea," Jeyra said.

Lotti wrinkled her nose and hesitated. "Maybe."

"We can't sit around and debate this. We need to get moving."

"I know."

"Then tell me. What is it?"

Lotti faced Jeyra and looked into her amber eyes. "The only way you'll get to the bottom of the lake is with magic."

"I assumed that. What's the problem?"

"I've never tried it before."

Jeyra grinned and winked at her. "What is that saying Varek keeps telling me when I succeed at things he shows me? Oh, right. *Beginner's luck*."

"Jeyra," Lotti began.

"I trust you. Besides, I can't die unless Varek does, remember?"

Lotti lowered her gaze to the dragon eye tattoo on Jeyra's left arm, just above her cuff—a mark every Dragon King mate bore. One that would grace Lotti's arm when she and Alasdair did the ceremony.

"I could still hurt you," Lotti said. "Unintentionally, of course."

Jeyra gently grabbed her by the shoulders. "You won't. Let's do this."

She turned and walked out of the forest before Lotti could stop her. She had no choice but to follow Jeyra. Lotti quickly caught up with her, praying Jeyra was right to be so confident about her abilities.

"I don't like being out in the open," Lotti murmured.

Jeyra's gaze swept the area around them. "All the more reason to move swiftly. How are we doing this?"

"I-I don't know." Lotti's mind raced with different ideas before settling on the easiest one. "Let's get into the water. Go under as soon as you can."

Jeyra didn't question her, she just did as Lotti suggested. Soon, they were both submerged in the shallows. Lotti grabbed Jeyra's hand and pulled her along as she dove. She reached the bottom about eight feet down, and the fractured light moved with the waves over the sand.

Lotti worked her legs, and Jeyra followed suit. Doubt assaulted Lotti. So many things could go wrong. Her magic could falter. Her idea might not work. Soldiers were coming after them. If she failed, they wouldn't reach the stone before Villette. It would be easy to give in to those misgivings, but then she looked to find Jeyra watching her. They couldn't hold their breaths forever. She had to act. Now.

Her magic worked simply by thinking of what she wanted. So, Lotti did just that and created a bubble between her hands. She grew the circle until it was large enough for both her and Jeyra to fit inside. It rested on the bottom of the lake like a huge sphere. She was the first to step through the viscous material. It clung to her for a heartbeat before she passed through entirely. The moment she could breathe, she motioned for Jeyra to join her.

Jeyra smiled as she dragged air into her lungs. "You're absolutely brilliant, Lotti."

"Let's just hope it holds up."

Jeyra gazed in wonder at the sphere that housed them and kept the water out. "How do we move it?"

"Walk."

To show her, Lotti began moving. The bubble rolled with them. Jeyra laughed and wiped water from her face.

An eel and several fish came close enough to investigate as they descended the slope. The deeper they went into the lake, the less light reached them until darkness soon surrounded them. Lotti held out her hands. When she did, light shone from them. But with every new solution, another problem arose.

The pressure from the water caused the sphere to wobble slightly. Lotti strengthened it, but her worry grew. Her attention was split between keeping the bubble sturdy and searching the dark water for the foot-long, milky orangish-pink massirine stone—large enough that it should stand out against the pale sand once light hit it.

"This could take hours," Jeyra murmured.

Lotti flattened her lips. "Or days."

"At least no one knows we're down here."

A shiver of dread ran down Lotti's spine the instant Jeyra said the words.

Jeyra glanced at her. "That way, we can look however long it takes."

"The boys will be worried if we don't surface soon."

"If they get away, they'll look for us. Two more pairs of eyes would be a great help."

Lotti looked out into the dark, murky water. "Aye, it would."

"What is it?"

"I don't know." Lotti swung her head to Jeyra. "Just a feeling."

Jeyra looked past her into the water. "I gather it isn't a good feeling."

"Nay."

"Then we'd better search faster."

Lotti moved them in a grid pattern to cover as much area as possible as the ground began sloping, getting steeper and steeper. With each passing moment, she hoped she would look up and see Alasdair swimming toward her. But he wasn't there. She and Jeyra were on their own. They had gotten through the forest and figured out a way to search for the stone. She told herself the uneasiness that plagued her was just the nagging fear of failing and nothing more.

"Shine the light over here," Jeyra called. "I thought I saw something glint."

Lotti shifted the light. As she did, she saw something large moving in the water.

Chapter Seven

Alasdair reared up on his hind legs when a large net came at his face, clamping around his nose and jaw tightly. Magic hummed through the fibers, and no amount of shaking his head removed it. Worse, he couldn't open his mouth to dislodge it. He clawed at the netting and continued to knock away soldiers with his tail and wings.

They had known exactly what he was. Their surprise had been genuine, however. That meant they hadn't been prepared to see a dragon so close. But their intentions were clear. They planned to capture him.

"Varek!"

"Give me a wee bit more time. More soldiers are headed to you."

Alasdair whipped his head around when he felt someone climb onto him. Enough was enough. Fury roiled as he glared at the men surrounding him. He finally managed to hook a talon between the mesh and his scales. He ripped it off with one yank. Pain bloomed everywhere the netting had touched. Alasdair tossed it at a group of soldiers and inwardly grinned when it trapped them. That gave him time to turn his attention to the man who had dared to climb up onto him. With a vicious shake, Alasdair dislodged the soldier. The man's shout of surprise as he fell was music to Alasdair's ears.

The soldiers were too busy attacking him to notice when darkness suddenly crept in from behind them. Within seconds, Varek's energy-draining shadows swallowed everyone. A heartbeat later, silence filled the forest again.

Varek's expression was grim as he walked from behind a tree. "I doona like this."

Alasdair returned to his human form. He stood naked in the woods, looking around at the unconscious soldiers before using his magic to clothe himself once more. "Villette knew I'd be here."

"We can no' linger."

"Let's take the net. I want a closer look at it since I felt its magic."

Varek stopped him with a hand on his arm. "There isna time. A group of soldiers is headed straight for us."

"Fuck," Alasdair grumbled.

Varek shot him a crooked grin. "What do you think? Do we find the girls, or stay and fight? We'll most likely have to kill. I know you purposely didna breathe fire because of the forest, but we'll need to use everything in our arsenal." He nodded at the netting. "Because they're going to continue their capture attempts."

Alasdair eyed the trees behind him. Now wasn't the time for a battle. That was coming soon enough. But they had to get the stone. And if Villette sent a second wave of soldiers, then she might have sent another to the lake. "We find the girls."

Without another word, they took off through the forest. Their preternatural speed allowed them to move swiftly, and they were no longer worried about being seen. Alasdair could see Varek out of the corner of his eye, ten feet away. The dragon within him demanded to be released. It made sense to return to his true form and reach the lake within moments so he could be with his mate, yet that would bring unwanted attention to them.

By sheer will alone, Alasdair kept himself in check. He knew Varek was likely also fighting that internal battle. Alasdair pumped his legs faster as fear reared its head and settled like a pit in his stomach. Images of all the ways Lotti could be harmed rattled through his mind in an endless stream of visions. He tried to remind himself that she could tap into unimaginable power, but it didn't dispel his panic. He and Varek were in such a hurry they didn't look for tracks. They were hedging everything on the fact that Lotti and Jeyra had reached the water.

The trees passed in a blur. Alasdair sprang over fallen trees and leapt down a steep drop, landing amid a pile of decaying leaves before continuing. He spotted another fallen tree up ahead. Varek vaulted over the huge trunk while Alasdair ran around the root ball that had been yanked from the ground.

Finally, he saw a glint of emerald water through the trees. Alasdair ran faster as he scanned the shoreline for Lotti. Something tackled him just as he was about to emerge from the forest. He rolled and rose up to loom over his attacker, ready to fight, only to find himself staring at Varek.

"What the hell?" Alasdair demanded.

Varek glared up at him. "You wouldna answer me. I had to stop you before you ran out." He took a breath and slowly released it. "We need to be careful."

Alasdair briefly closed his eyes as he stood and pulled Varek up. "Sorry, brother. I only had one thought."

"Aye. I have the same one about Jeyra, but we willna do either of them any good if we rush into a trap."

Alasdair faced the water. It was long and narrow, hence the name *Narrow Lake*. "I doona see them."

"Let's look for tracks. If they made it to the water, there will be evidence."

Alasdair pulled his gaze from the shore and began scouting the ground for tracks. Varek went in one direction, and he headed in the other. Alasdair decided the easiest way to locate footprints was to look along the forest's edge. He searched the area, slowly working his way down the tree line, acutely aware that neither Lotti nor Jeyra was standing at the lake's edge.

It would be easy to fall back into the circle of dread that had plagued him on the run here. It was stupid to berate himself for not being with them, but love had a way of making a man crazy with gut-wrenching fear and the overwhelming need to protect and defend those he cared about.

"Alasdair."

He whirled around at the sound of Varek's voice and rushed to his friend. Alasdair looked down to where Varek pointed and found two sets of tracks. Relief poured through him so quickly that he had to grab a tree to stay upright.

Varek grinned and slapped him on the back. "I knew they'd make it."

Alasdair's smile died as his gaze swung to the lake. "Then where are they?"

"My guess is underwater."

"Or captured."

Varek shook his head with a wry grin. "You need to trust Lotti to take care of herself, brother."

"I do."

Varek's deep brown eyes met his. "Then why does your mind go to the worst possible theory?"

"You were no' there. You didna battle your dead brother or watch your mate face off with beings so powerful they could defeat us."

Varek pressed his lips together. "Nay, I wasna. But Lotti was. She survived. As did you. She *is* one of those formidable beings."

"You're telling me you're no' worried about Jeyra?"

"Every fucking second of every day. I fight no' to let it control me. It's a battle I wage each time we face off against our enemies."

"Does it get easier?"

Varek smiled wryly. "No' even after the mating ceremony. She lets me know if she needs my help. Until that time, I fight beside her."

It was good advice. Alasdair gave his friend a nod of thanks.

"Ready for a swim?" Varek asked.

"There hasna been any movement in the forest, around the shore, or in the water."

"Let's hope that means Villette hasna sent anyone here yet. Maybe she believes all she needed was the trap in the woods."

Alasdair grunted. "I doubt it. Villette is shrewd and calculating. She has plenty of soldiers to spread around the area to watch for us, including at both lakes."

"What do you want to do?"

It was about fifty feet from the tree line to the edge of the lake. He eyed the mountains on the other side of the body of water, pausing when he saw the cliff Lotti had mentioned. "Find the girls. I'd rather face off against anything that comes at us together."

"I agree. That's our best bet."

"Then let's go swimming."

They walked out of the forest and across the sand to the water's edge. Alasdair paused to look at the sky. Then he dove into the lake after Varek. The water was clear and cool as they swam beneath the surface. They stayed within eyesight of each other while searching for any sign of the girls or the stone.

It wasn't long before they were so deep the sun could no longer penetrate the water. Since dragons could see as well in the dark as they could in the light, it wasn't an issue for Alasdair or Varek. But it would be for the girls.

Alasdair kicked his feet faster. He saw the usual aquatic animals. They weren't exactly like those on Earth, but they were similar enough that he knew what they were. A school of fish darted around and between him and Varek, swimming away quickly. He caught sight of a dark-scaled fish nearly his size, but it was content to keep its distance.

The descent to the bottom of the lake was probably two thousand feet. The depth surprised Alasdair. And troubled him. Though, everything seemed to worry him lately. He hadn't been like this before, and he hoped he got a handle on it soon.

Varek slowed to investigate something before continuing. Alasdair wondered how the girls were staying beneath the water since they couldn't hold their breaths for that long. Both women were resourceful, though. They would've thought of something. A small portion of his knot of worry loosened.

A flash caught Alasdair's attention. He focused on the direction and waited. It wasn't long before he saw it again. A smile split his face as he realized it was a light, which meant it was most likely the girls.

"Varek, this way. I think I found them," Alasdair said.

They began swimming toward the light. As they drew closer, Alasdair saw the large sphere resting on the lake bottom, holding Lotti and Jeyra. The illumination came from Lotti's hands. Just as he figured. Resourceful.

They didn't want to scare the girls, so he and Varek swam around the globe. Lotti was the first to see them. Her smile was huge as she met his gaze. Both girls began talking excitedly while pointing at something. Alasdair followed the direction of their hands. He swam forward for a closer look and caught sight of the edge of the massirine stone sticking out of the sand.

Not only had the girls' plan to get to the lake worked, but they'd also found the stone. Now, all they had to do was retrieve it and return to Iron Hall. Alasdair thought about the soldiers who'd attacked him, as well as the army headed their way. They might have to find another way home, but at least they were together. That's what mattered.

The sphere moved as Lotti and Jeyra walked closer to the stone. He and Varek attempted to hold it in place. It wasn't easy because their hands kept going through it. Jeyra reached her arm through the ball and into the water. Her fingers sank into the sand as she craned her head away from the sphere and searched by touch. Alasdair mentally urged her to shift to the side when her fingers missed the stone by half an inch. He grunted when she moved in the wrong direction. Varek positioned himself in front of her and directed her as best he could.

Jeyra adjusted her position and tried again. Her fingers brushed the stone but couldn't grasp it in time before the globe shifted slightly. Alasdair and Varek steadied the bubble once more while Jeyra turned to the side to allow more of her arm to extend. Varek used his hand to guide hers to the domed stone. Everyone held their breath when her fingers latched on to it, and she tugged it free of the sand and then pulled it into the sphere.

Alasdair and Varek shared a smile while the girls celebrated their victory. Alasdair was about to suggest that he and Varek haul the sphere up with them when Lotti looked past him, her eyes widening in fear.

Alasdair turned and found himself looking into his brother's citrine eyes. Without hesitation, he shoved the globe away just as Gordon reached for it with his claws.

Chapter Eight

The sight of the dragon behind Alasdair paralyzed Lotti. The memory of their last battle on the snowy mountain filled her head—along with terror. Something shoved the sphere, causing her to lose her footing. She fell hard on her side just as the globe started to roll. Lotti frantically searched for Alasdair and saw him shift before she and Jeyra were tumbling inside the bubble as it bounced across the lake bed.

Lotti fought to gain her feet and stop the ball from rolling. Each time she got close to standing, she was knocked on her bum once more. Fear consumed her. Not for herself, but for Alasdair. And that prevented her from quieting her mind and controlling the sphere. Lotti doused the light from her palms and focused all her energy on halting the bubble. It rocked slightly when it finally came to rest on the lakebed once more. Only then did she release a sigh.

She shoved her hair out of her eyes and looked over. She could hear Jeyra, but she couldn't see her. "Are you all right?"

"Ask me later," Jeyra whispered. "That was…that was…"

Lotti understood her distress. "Gordon."

"Shite. Well, at least we have the stone."

"We need to get to the surface."

Jeyra made a noise. "I think we're better off staying right here. It's two against one out there. Varek and Alasdair will make quick work of Gordon. How did he know we were here?"

"Your guess is as good as mine."

A startled yelp fell from Lotti's lips as something violently slammed into the sphere and sent them rolling once more. She landed on Jeyra. Lotti winced as Jeyra's elbow connected with her temple and something else jammed into her ribs. Lotti stopped the bubble quicker this time, but they were both still reeling.

Lotti moved off Jeyra, hoping she didn't accidentally touch the stone in the process. She stood on unsteady legs and spread out her arms, attempting to keep the sphere from being moved again.

"I really don't like when that happens," Jeyra mumbled.

Lotti hoped her friend wasn't hurt. She wanted to see, but she didn't like splitting her power. Remaining still was more important than being able to see. Besides, the dragons could see them in the dark. The only ones hampered were her and Jeyra.

"Um...Lotti. We have a problem."

Her heart sank as she turned her head toward Jeyra's voice. She feared she already knew the problem before asking. "What is it?"

"Water is dripping above me."

"I was afraid of that." The pressure had already caused issues, but that last hit must have done even more damage. Lotti closed her eyes and focused on repairing the damage. She could do this. If she doubted herself, she could doom them both. "I'm fixing it."

"Lotti!"

Jeyra's frightened shout made Lotti's eyes fly open. She jerked back at the sight of fire rushing toward them. A large form blocked it just before the flames encircled the bubble. Lotti glimpsed amethyst scales before the light died away.

"We can't stay here," Jeyra said.

Lotti heard bodies clashing and the occasional roar outside of the sphere. The water dampened some of the noise, but not all of it. She licked her lips. "Hold on."

She began lifting the bubble from the lake bottom. Water surged and churned as she hoisted them as fast as she dared. But their escape was cut short when talons pierced the sphere, and water gushed in.

"Jeyra!" Lotti shouted, reaching for her.

Within seconds, her magic disintegrated. Lotti desperately tried to create another bubble for them, but her attention was split between searching for Jeyra, wondering if Gordon was coming for her, and using her magic. The more divided her mind, the more her powers seized.

Another round of dragon fire blinded her. The blaze was intense, even underwater, as it roiled and grew. She used the opportunity to look for Jeyra. Lotti found her struggling against the water pressure when another dragon, this one with lichen-colored scales, raced to her. Varek's large hand gently scooped Jeyra against him as he scrambled for the surface.

Lotti saw the rush of bubbles coming at her in time to duck before a large tail collided with her. She lifted her head and watched as Gordon raced after Varek and Jeyra. To Lotti's relief, Alasdair shot past her, his hand outstretched to grab Gordon's tail. Her lungs began to burn from holding her breath. She could think about being on shore and be there in the next heartbeat, but she needed to help her friends.

She imagined herself at the surface. A second later, she was there—just in time to see Varek breach the water. His wings spread to take flight as water sluiced down his scales. Abruptly, Gordon yanked him back into the lake. Violent waves slammed into Lotti as she tried to keep her eyes on Varek and Jeyra.

Lotti couldn't tell if he still had a hold of Jeyra or not, but she didn't see Jeyra in the water. Which meant Varek must have her. Lotti needed to do something. Maybe she could get Varek free. Gordon let out a deafening roar and raked his talons down Varek's scales. Then Alasdair was there. He charged from the water and yanked Gordon away, pulling him beneath the surface.

"Go now!" Lotti screamed to Varek.

She watched as he flew into the sky and headed toward Iron Hall. Lotti dove under the water, intent on finding Alasdair. She found him and Gordon locked together, rolling through the water while clawing and biting at each other. They moved so quickly that Lotti couldn't tell the brothers apart. She could use her magic, but she didn't want to mistakenly strike Alasdair.

Lotti got her chance when they broke apart. She didn't hesitate to send a wave of magic directly at Gordon. It struck him in the side and spun him away. He floated, stunned. The next thing Lotti knew, Alasdair was beside her. His jade dragon eyes met hers, and he held out his hand before glancing at Gordon. Lotti settled her palm against his. He closed his fingers around hers, and they shot through the water in the next instant.

Lotti couldn't see where they were headed. She hoped she'd stunned Gordon long enough for them to get away. Squeezing her eyes closed, she prayed Jeyra was unhurt. Had Gordon been in the water with them the entire time? Had he been waiting to strike until they had the stone? Or had he waited for Alasdair? How had Gordon even known they were in the lake? But she knew the answer.

Villette.

She was so lost in thought she was slow to realize that Alasdair had stopped. A moment later, her head was above water. His hand opened, and she found herself treading water in a darkened room.

A warm body moved against hers. She recognized the large hands and strong arms that pulled her against his length. Lotti wound her arms around Alasdair's neck and held him as he treaded water. They stayed like that for a moment, Lotti lost in thought of what had happened—and what was to come—Alasdair likely thinking the same. Then he tugged her after him as he swam.

"Where are we?" she asked, trying to see into the darkness.

"I saw an opening in the wall of the lake," Alasdair said.

Lotti frowned. "How did you know it went anywhere?"

"I didna. With Gordon stunned, we had a chance to get away. Thank you for that, by the way."

She grinned. "Anytime. Why not fly us after Varek?"

"Because that's exactly what my brother will think we did."

She brushed against rock and latched on to it when Alasdair released her. The sound of water dripping from his body filled the silence as he climbed out. Then his hands wrapped around her wrists to lift her onto solid ground. At almost the same time, a light bloomed over them.

Lotti looked up at the warm glow before meeting Alasdair's gaze. "Maybe we should be with Varek and Jeyra to help protect the stone."

"By the time Gordon goes after them, they'll be on dragon land and far out of his reach."

"You've spoken with Varek?"

Alasdair's lips flattened. "I can no' get through."

She leaned against Alasdair and pressed her face to his bare chest, soaking in the warmth of his body. "Villette was prepared for every action we took. What if she planned for one of us getting away?"

"Cullen is waiting if there's a problem. He'll get Varek and Jeyra."

"I believed we had taken every precaution to stay far from Villette."

Alasdair rubbed his hands up and down her back against her wet clothes. "She has an army at her disposal. Besides, we couldna plan for every eventuality."

She looked at the stone wall and realized they were within a mountain. Lotti shivered, as much from the chill as knowing how close they were to Villette.

"Come," Alasdair said. "Let's rest while we can. I want to hear what happened with you and Jeyra, and I'll share about my and Varek's encounter."

Lotti let him lead her farther from the water. Her gaze moved over his muscular body, taking in his wide shoulders that tapered to a narrow waist, then roaming over his tight bum to his corded thighs. A fire suddenly blazed to life, and thick blankets covered the floor. She looked at Alasdair as a different kind of fire started within her.

He shrugged and grinned. "You're no' the only one with impressive magic."

She knew he was attempting to take her mind off their situation, and she appreciated the effort. Lotti dried her clothes with a thought. Alasdair sat, leaning against a rock wall. He patted the space between his legs. She took a moment to admire the dragon tattoo covering his chest. The black and red ink was a beautiful combination, but it paled in comparison to the design itself.

The dragon sat in the middle of his chest with its large wings spread and its head nestled between Alasdair's collarbones, gazing up at Alasdair. The dragon's tail hung and then curled near Alasdair's right hip bone. She had traced that dragon many times as they lay together, and she knew she would never tire of looking at it.

"Come, lass," Alasdair beckoned.

She removed her boots and sank to the ground.

"There are many openings like this cave in the lake," Alasdair said as he wrapped his arms around her and tenderly drew her back against his chest.

Lotti gripped his arms. "I never would've thought to look for anything like this."

"You were pretty incredible today, you know."

"I didn't do nearly enough."

"You created a sphere to take you and Jeyra to the bottom of the lake. Do you have any idea how deep that was?"

She shrugged. "Deep."

"Aye. Verra. You also struck Gordon, allowing us to escape."

She shrugged. "I did what I had to do."

"How did you breathe under the water?"

Lotti frowned as she shook her head. "I...I don't think I did."

"You must have. I swam as fast as I could, but the pressure alone should've made things difficult for you."

"I was so worried about getting away and joining Jeyra and Varek that I didn't even think. Alasdair...do you think I can...?" She couldn't finish the sentence.

He kissed her temple. "Aye, lass. I do."

"I'm not sure what to think about that."

"Then doona. You've learned you can do something else. Just accept it."

"It isn't that easy sometimes."

He rested his chin atop her head. "I imagine it isna."

"We can stop Villette, can't we? We have to. There isn't another option."

"Aye, love. We'll stop her."

"Good. Now, tell me what happened with you and Varek."

Lotti listened as Alasdair detailed the attack and the soldiers who prevented them from getting to their rendezvous location. She was furious to learn about the netting and the additional soldiers coming up behind Alasdair and Varek.

Alasdair shrugged. "So, we came straight to you and Jeyra."

"It's a good thing you did," Lotti said. "I wouldn't have wanted to battle Gordon alone."

"I think you could've handled him all on your own."

She grunted, wanting to believe him but unsure of her abilities. "That net they used on you makes me uneasy."

"Aye. It is concerning. The difference between our other enemies and Villette is that she knows dragons like few do. She knows our strengths and weaknesses. That's why she seems to guess our every move."

Lotti turned her head to the side to see him. "That doesn't explain how she knew where we would go."

"I doona think she did. She used her army to watch over a wide swath of area. Think about it. Stonemore conquered villages and other cities for years, bringing the people into Stonemore. It's why it's so overpopulated and people are starving. However, with every conquest, Villette broadens her army. Whether to use it for war or something like today, she has a nearly endless supply of soldiers at her beck and call."

Lotti closed her eyes and faced forward. "We didn't kill anyone today, but we won't always be able to say that."

"Varek and I tried no' to take any lives, but I can no' guarantee no one died."

"That has to count for something."

He grunted. "I'm no' sure the other side will see it that way. Today, they met their greatest adversary, an enemy they despise above all others. Me. Some ran, but the ones who remained had such hatred in their eyes it was startling."

"We have to change their way of thinking."

"I fear it's too deeply ingrained."

Lotti stretched her feet toward the fire, letting the flames warm her. "We won't know unless we try."

"Aye, that's true. Now, tell me about getting to the lake. I want to know every detail."

"First, Jeyra is fearless and remarkable."

Alasdair chuckled. "So are you, love."

Lotti took a breath and began her tale.

Chapter Nine

Alasdair held Lotti, feeling the breath move through her as she slept. He hadn't released her. It had taken great effort not to yank her against him when they arrived in the cave. He'd attempted to keep his composure and must have pulled it off because she hadn't said anything to the contrary.

But alone with his thoughts now, he gave in to the riotous emotions battering him. His eyes closed as he remembered how Gordon had burst the sphere. The utter terror that consumed Alasdair had stopped his heart. Then rage took hold.

When he fought his long-dead brother on top of the mountain, he had been trying to defeat Gordon and get to Lotti. Now, all Alasdair wanted to do was end Gordon before he could take the life of Lotti or another in his family.

Alasdair blinked open his eyes and swallowed as emotion choked him. He knew just how close they had come to disaster. Gordon's strength now superseded what he'd possessed as a Dragon King. That dragon might be using Gordon's body, but it wasn't his brother. The might and power Gordon exuded were cause for concern. The next time they fought, Alasdair would have to come at it a different way.

Gordon hadn't hesitated to fight both him and Varek. Granted, Varek's goal had been to grab Jeyra and get free. Things might have been different had Gordon faced off against both of them at once. The fact remained that Gordon wasn't going anywhere. At least not until Alasdair killed him. Again.

He had never wanted to fight his brother, but Earth's magic had declared Gordon unworthy of being the King of Amethysts. It chose Alasdair for the position, and that meant there was only one solution: a fight to the death.

Alasdair was plagued by nightmares for centuries afterward. Gordon had been his brother, his blood. He might have become a twisted version of the dragon Alasdair knew and loved, but Gordon was still family at the core. Still, the clan's fate rested on Alasdair's shoulders, giving him no choice. Now, he was battling his brother all over again.

It was a living hell.

Lotti stirred in his arms, rolling her head to the other side before settling. Her power was new, and Alasdair told himself that was why he was so overprotective. The truth wasn't as simple. He had seen how capable she was. With each new dangerous situation, Lotti didn't just come through, she surpassed anything she had done previously. The simple fact was that her abilities were nearly limitless.

Yet there was always a kernel of fear that she could be taken from him. He never imagined he could love anyone as unconditionally and absolutely as he did Lotti. He had seen the love between his fellow Kings and their mates and knew how strong and resolute that bond could be. But he hadn't truly known its impact until Lotti. She changed everything. And he didn't want that taken from him.

Clinging to her and their love wasn't the way to face their challenges. Varek had urged him to trust Lotti's decisions and power. Alasdair claimed he did, but that wasn't exactly true. And that had to change. She didn't need his protection. He had to let her become the force he felt when he absorbed her magic. He knew better than most what she was capable of because he had experienced the dominance of her raw power—the potency and command—when he used it with his while in the mountain at Stonemore.

Alasdair released a long breath as his gaze settled on the dark water. There were two ways out for them—the lake or the mountain. He wasn't pleased with either. Especially since he couldn't reach Varek or any of the Kings.

So, he waited—something he didn't do well.

His thoughts halted when Lotti took a deep breath and rubbed her hands down his arms. He pressed his face against the side of her head. She reached back and touched his cheek.

"Do you know what I just realized?" she asked sleepily.

"What's that?"

"We keep ending up back within mountains."

His lips widened into a grin. "Aye, we do."

"Maybe it's telling us something."

"It? Meaning the mountain?"

She shrugged. "Perhaps. It could be fate or destiny."

"And what is it telling us?"

"That we're meant to be here. Think about it," she said, sitting up and turning to face him. "Last time you spoke to Merrill, we learned about the stone and what Stonemore was using it for, and we uncovered that Villette is the Divine."

He pulled hair from her lashes. "Doona forget that you also discovered who you are."

"As well as what my people did to yours."

"That has nothing to do with you."

"It has everything to do with me," she replied.

Alasdair shook his head. "How can it? You were no' even born, love."

"Some won't see the difference."

"I do. My family does. We're the ones who count. Ignore everyone else."

She rose to her knees and straddled him. His cock hardened as she flattened her hands on his chest. Heat infused Alasdair, the kind only Lotti could stir. Desire licked at him, growing with each heartbeat.

Her hands caressed up his shoulders to his neck and then moved to his face. Turquoise eyes held his. "I love you."

"I love you," he murmured, sitting up and splaying his hands on her back.

Their lips met, sending a flare of need roaring through him. He slid his tongue past her lips to tangle with hers. She sucked in a breath and wound her arms around his neck. His balls tightened as her breasts pressed against him. He would never get his fill of this woman. He burned for her and her alone.

He deepened the kiss, becoming lost in all that was Lotti. She moaned into his mouth when he held her hips and ground against her. Then he was clawing at her clothes to remove them. Suddenly, the material was gone, and only flesh met his hands.

Alasdair kissed down her throat as she moved sensually against him. Each time her slick heat met his aching cock, the desire intensified. He slid his hands over the swells of her hips to the indent of her waist and then moved higher until he cupped her breasts. She sighed, her chest heaving. He massaged the globes as he stared in wonder at the pleasure that crossed her face. Then he turned his focus to the turgid peaks begging for attention.

"Aye," she said in a breathy voice when he teased her nipples.

Her head dropped back, pushing her breasts toward him. He lowered his head and wrapped his lips around one peak then gently pulled. Her nails dug into his shoulders. The action only spurred him on, urging him to heighten her pleasure. He used his mouth, tongue, and fingers to tease her breasts. As her breathing became ragged, her hips rocked faster against the length of his arousal. She was wet and ready for him.

He wanted to be inside her, but first, he planned to bring her to climax at least twice. Alasdair fought against the lure of her sex as he grabbed her hips and lifted her. For just a moment, he almost gave in and settled her on his rod.

* * * *

Lotti tried to lower herself onto Alasdair. She needed his thick cock inside her, filling her as only he could. But he held her firmly. Then she was on her back as he loomed over her. Need darkened his eyes and tightened his face. She reached for him, and their lips came together in a rush of yearning.

She rocked her hips against his hard body and moaned at the delicious sensations rocketing through her. A moan tore from her throat when he shifted, and his chest brushed against her sensitive nipples. Her sex clenched greedily. She tried to reach for his arousal, but he caught her wrists and held them out to the sides, pinning her beneath him.

Alasdair's chest heaved as he gazed at her hungrily. Then he trailed kisses down her neck to her breasts. She bit her lip when his tongue circled a nipple before moving to the other. She pushed her chest out, eager for him. The corners of his eyes crinkled slightly when he met her gaze right before sucking her other nipple deep into his mouth.

Every nerve ending was alight with pleasure. She raised her hips, seeking contact, needing the pressure against his body. Lotti moaned in frustration when she couldn't get it. Then his mouth trailed a string of hot kisses between her breasts and down her stomach. His tongue circled her belly button before moving to her hip. He continued across to her other hip with agonizing slowness. She didn't move, eager to have his mouth on her center.

He released his hold on her wrists, and she immediately reached for him. She gripped the thick sinew of his arms, silently willing him to give her the release she so desperately needed, but also wanting to prolong the pleasure.

She closed her eyes and gave herself over to the swarm of sensations rolling through her. She was acutely aware of Alasdair's mouth. When he moved close to her center, she held her breath, only to release it when he kissed up the inner thigh of her right leg. He continued his teasing by shifting to the left and repeating the action.

Her sex throbbed impatiently. There was no use begging. Alasdair would move at his own pace. And if she tried to hurry him, he would only take longer.

She sank into the fur blankets, a low moan filling the area when his tongue slowly ran over her center. A soft cry left her the instant he found her clit. She spread her legs wider, and he settled between them.

He brought her to the brink in seconds and easily held her there. Lotti was about to beg for release when he slid a finger inside her, finding that perfect spot. She gasped, her back arching as she rode his hand. Desire twisted tighter and tighter until it shattered with her orgasm.

* * * *

No matter how many times he felt her body spasm around his fingers or cock, Alasdair could never get enough. He kept up his ministrations until her body went lax. Even then, the walls of her sex continued to contract with the last vestiges of her climax.

He withdrew his fingers and rose over her. He could no longer deny his body. He flipped her onto her hands and knees, and she looked at him over her shoulder and gave him a look filled with need. He guided his rod to her entrance and slid inside. She moaned loudly before pushing back against him.

Alasdair held her hips and began thrusting hard and deep. He kept a steady rhythm, and soon, she was moaning. Her wet heat enveloped him again and again, pushing him closer to release. He came the moment he felt the walls of her body shuddering around him. He gripped her firmly and buried himself deep as she milked him of every last drop.

They stayed locked together for several moments as their breathing evened out. Then he pulled out of her. Lotti lay on her back and tugged him down beside her. They lay together, staring at the ceiling of the cave.

He rose and leaned on one elbow to look at her, running a finger along her cheek to her jaw. He was as taken with her beauty now as he had been when he first saw her. She suddenly smiled up at him, causing his lips to curve into a grin.

"See? I told you we were meant for mountains," she teased.

His heart swelled for her. "So it would seem."

"What do we do now? We should probably figure a way out."

"No' yet," he murmured as he lowered his head. "I have other plans," he finished before kissing her.

Chapter Ten

Lotti would happily stay in Alasdair's arms for eternity if she could. He had come into her life and shown her he was as solid and unmovable as the mountains. He shouldered her burdens without a second thought. All those decades she had wandered alone, forever watching others but never being a part of anything, had taken a toll. The loneliness itself had left scars, cutting deeper than any blade could.

Alasdair had changed all of that. He'd gained her trust, and with that, she'd learned not to fear her magic but to embrace it, accept it. It had been so simple. Her life could've been different had she done it years earlier. But the past was the past. There was no use looking over her shoulder and questioning her choices. It was time to be in the present.

And that meant finding a way out of the cave.

She closed her eyes as Alasdair's fingers drifted lazily along her spine as she lay curled against his side. They could pretend the outside world, with all its dangers and threats, couldn't reach them in the cave. It was a distraction they'd both needed, but it was time to get back to reality.

"I ken," Alasdair murmured.

Lotti grinned at his deep voice and accent so different from anything she had ever heard on Zora. He had promised to take her to see his home in Scotland one day, and she couldn't wait. "Reading my mind again?" she teased.

He kissed the top of her head. "I doona think that's a gift I'd ever wish to have. I heard you sigh and know your thoughts are running along the same vein as mine."

"We need to get back to Iron Hall."

"Aye."

She inhaled deeply and released it as she rose onto her elbow to look at him. "What does it say about me that I don't want to leave this place?"

His gaze was tender as he gently smoothed her hair away from her face. "It doesna say anything, love. I doona wish to leave either."

"Do you think there will ever come a time when we're not fighting someone trying to harm the Kings or dragons?"

"Or those with magic," he added. Alasdair shrugged and looked at the ceiling. "I'd love to say there will be, but the truth is that I doona know. We had times of peace on Earth, but nothing lasts forever."

She leaned forward to kiss him, her lips lingering. Then she looked down at him again. "Then there's only one thing for us to do."

"And what's that?"

"Fight when we must. And when we have peace, embrace every moment we're given."

Alasdair's lips curved. "Doona forget the occasions we snatch for ourselves."

"Never," she said with a smile.

It would be so easy to kiss him again and give in to the desire once more, but they had taken as much time as they could. Lotti got to her feet and grabbed her clothes. She could have redressed in an instant, just as she'd removed everything earlier, but she wanted the time to consider their options.

She tucked the shirt into her body-skimming pants and fastened the leather vest that fit snuggly against her torso. Lotti sat on a boulder to put on her boots that reached her knees. Alasdair was already dressed in his all-black attire. He leaned a shoulder against the wall with his arms crossed, his gaze on her.

"How do you make everything so bloody sexy?" he asked.

Her stomach fluttered at the heat she saw in his eyes. She stood and grinned. "Just lucky, I guess. So," she said, looking at the water, "do we go back the way we came?"

"We could."

She swung her gaze to him. "You'd rather go through the mountain?"

"I doona think either of our routes is better than the other. Gordon could be waiting for us, just as he was before. Even if he followed Varek and Jeyra, he most likely returned to the lake."

"And you don't want to fight him again."

"Nay, I doona." Alasdair pushed away from the wall, dropping his arms. "I had to take my brother's life once already. I doona relish doing it again. But I know I'll have to. He's stronger than before—as strong as a King, which shouldna be possible."

"He was once a Dragon King."

"And he shouldna be here. Whatever Villette did to bring him back must have changed him."

Lotti's stomach twisted as it did each time they discussed Gordon. "We may never know what she did."

"We need to learn, though. No' only that, we need to know if she brought back other dragons. I just doona understand why she chose Gordon."

"We could spend an eternity trying to discern that and never learn anything."

Alasdair nodded and blew out a breath. "You're right. I need to stop fixating on it."

"It's your brother. Anyone would be consumed by those questions."

"That doesna get us out of here."

Lotti swallowed. It was time for her suggestion. "What if I can get us home?"

"What do you mean?"

"Remember when Villette attacked me while you were battling Gordon the first time? Eurielle told me I just needed to think about what I wanted to make it happen. When Villette dropped me over the cliff, I stopped myself and landed safely. I did the same when we were in the water earlier. I was at the bottom and wanted to be at the top, and then…I was. I think I can get us back to Iron Hall the same way."

Alasdair considered her words. "That's a considerably greater distance than what you've tried. Fae can teleport. There are even pieces of jewelry that allow whoever wears them to jump from one place to another."

"So, it can be done."

"But you've no' tried it before."

"Not yet."

"I'm no' sure now is the time."

Lotti understood his hesitation. She was still learning, but she would never know unless she tried. "You think Erith is one of the Star People. Can she teleport?"

"She can."

"We know Villette and Eurielle can, too. Doesn't it stand to reason that I would be able to?"

Alasdair walked to her and rested his hands on her upper arms. "I doona question whether you can. I'm simply asking if I should be tagging along the first time you try it."

"How else am I going to get us back if I don't take you with me?"

"Try and see if you can do it alone. If you can, then come back for me."

"All right."

He slid his hand down her arm and linked his fingers with hers, giving them a squeeze before stepping away. "Give it a go."

Excitement surged through Lotti. She had all these incredible powers, and she had a quick solution that would keep them out of harm's way. She had been waiting for this moment since the second she learned who she was. One where she could show everyone that she was capable of helping them.

Lotti closed her eyes and thought about Iron Hall—the main chamber with the pool and the tree. Yet she didn't move. She tried again, focusing on a particular spot in the hidden city. When that didn't work, Lotti switched locations and thought about the chamber that she and Alasdair had chosen as theirs.

"I don't understand why it isn't working," she said in disbelief.

Alasdair's voice was calm and soothing when he said, "Doona be so hard on yourself. You've never attempted such a thing before."

She should have. She should have been trying everything to learn what she could and couldn't do. Lotti shook her head and gave up. "I'm sorry."

"Doona apologize." Alasdair took her hands in his. "Just because you can no' do it now doesna mean you willna in the future."

But it would've been helpful now. She forced a smile she didn't feel. "I know."

"Water or cave?"

Lotti looked at the dark waves. The lake was vast, giving Gordon many places to hide. Even if she and Alasdair got out of the water without incident, they still had to get through the forest. Unless, of course, he flew them home. Varek had done that. The Kings were doing their best to keep out of the skies, but she could cloak them again so no one saw them.

She turned to the dark tunnel that lay behind the light above them. They could find a way through quickly. Then again, they could be locked within the mountain and find themselves once again close to Villette.

"Either way, we risk encountering enemies," she finally said. "We know what to expect if we go back the way we came."

Alasdair's lips twisted, and he shrugged. "Verra true. They'll be looking for us. If we take another route, we could avoid any confrontations."

"What is that adage Cullen says? The odds of that are slim to none?"

Alasdair chuckled. "Point taken. The truth is that both options have pros and cons. We're liable to run into trouble whichever choice we make."

"I say we take our chances in the lake. Once we're out, I'll cloak us, and you can fly us to Iron Hall. It won't matter if Villette is searching for magic. She already knows we're here."

"I agree. Besides, being outside gives us options that a narrow tunnel doesna. I didna shift when we were in Stonemore because I didna want the crumbling mountain to take any lives. I willna have that concern out there."

"Good point." Lotti faced the water. "Let's go home."

They jumped into the waves together. Alasdair pulled her down into the depths before shifting. She knew he was just being cautious, but she was glad he was in his true form. He didn't hold her in his palm this time. Lotti released her grip on his hand and hung in the water as he swam beneath her. She then grabbed hold of one of the amethyst growths atop his head and cloaked them. The instant she had a firm grip, he tucked his wings tightly against him and sped forward.

Bubbles exploded all around them, blocking her view. He twisted and turned through the underwater tunnel. Lotti could feel her heart beating in her chest from the adrenaline. She didn't have to hold her breath, but she couldn't breathe underwater either. She simply was. Another thing raising a question in a long list of things she didn't understand about herself.

Alasdair followed the passageway as it dropped down at a steep pitch. The shaft leveled out eventually and stayed that way for a considerable distance. Then, finally, he angled his body upward. They shot from the cave like an arrow. The expanse of dark water around them caused a chill to snake down Lotti's spine. She and Jeyra had entered the lake without thought of anything lurking beneath the surface. Now, she knew better. Unfortunately, everywhere she looked was a possible hiding place for any number of threats.

She tightened her grip when Alasdair propelled them straight up, ducking her head against the force of the water. Every so often, she chanced a look to either side of her. It didn't matter that they were cloaked. Anyone would be able to see the movement of the water and the bubbles.

During one of those glances, she noticed sunlight through the water. They were nearly to the surface. Lotti smiled. All they needed was to get out of the lake and everything would be fine.

No sooner had the thought gone through her mind than Alasdair's head breached the surface. At nearly the same instant, something rammed them from underneath. Lotti saw a large talon coming at her. Alasdair jerked, and she lost her hold, plummeting back into the lake.

Chapter Eleven

Alasdair knew the instant Lotti let go. His heart clenched, and there was a moment where he fought the need to get to her instead of battling Gordon. Then he remembered she was powerful and clever. She would be all right. Once he did that, the vise around his chest loosened, and he turned the full force of his rage on the dragon who had once been his brother.

He swiped at Gordon with his talons, catching on his scales. Alasdair sank his claws deep, letting them cut through the wide plates until Gordon roared in pain and anger. His brother's retaliation was swift. Alasdair leaned away, the water making it difficult to dodge the combination of snapping teeth and the tail wrapping firmly around his back leg.

Alasdair's head jerked back from the impact of Gordon ramming him under the chin. Stars dotted his vision as he was yanked beneath the water. Alasdair still had a hold of his brother, and he sank his talons in deeper. Gordon clamped a hand around Alasdair's neck, his citrine eyes blazing with hatred.

If there had been any doubt that this wasn't his brother, it vanished instantly. Even when he and Gordon had battled to the death for the position of King of Amethysts, there had been no hatred in his brother's eyes—acceptance and even relief, but never animosity.

Alasdair used his tail to lash at Gordon while being pulled ever downward. He didn't know what Gordon planned, and it didn't matter. He was getting back to Lotti and going home. Jeyra and Varek had the massirine stone, which meant they had scored a crucial blow against Villette.

Blood colored the water. Alasdair didn't know how much of it was his. Both he and Gordon had pierced scales. Battle was part of a dragon's life—or it had been. Once the Kings sent the dragons away, they only had each other. They fought the Fae and anyone else who dared to target them or Earth, but engaging with another dragon wasn't the same.

Alasdair clenched his teeth and peeled back his lips as Gordon's talons cut through muscle and scraped against bone.

* * * *

Lotti hurried toward shore as water ran in thick rivulets down her clothes and body. She swiped at the hair that clung to her face to get it away from her eyes and spun around, searching for Alasdair.

Waves crashed around her from the vicious battle before Alasdair and Gordon disappeared beneath the water. She panted from her exertion and apprehension. Her gaze moved back and forth across the lake. The longer she went without seeing Alasdair, the more troubled she became. He was a Dragon King. He didn't need her help. But that didn't mean she wouldn't give it. If he didn't come up soon, she would go back into the water after him. He had told her multiple times that he didn't want to kill Gordon again. She would do it for him. Then she was going after Villette to end all of this.

Lotti took a step deeper into the shallows. Water swirled around her calves as waves rose as high as her thighs before slamming into the shore. She was done waiting. She was going after Alasdair.

A sound caught her attention. She turned her head toward the woods but didn't see anyone. She took another step and was about to dive beneath the surface when she heard her name. Lotti looked at the trees once more. This time, a shape came out of the forest.

"Jeyra?" Lotti whispered in shock when she saw her friend's torn clothes and the blood on her face.

The redheaded warrior dropped to her knees.

* * * *

Alasdair knew if he didn't get away from Gordon soon, he likely never would. He couldn't tell if his brother was attempting to trap or kill him. It didn't matter which one Gordon intended. Alasdair wouldn't allow either.

His tail repeatedly lashed at Gordon, striking his brother's back and legs. Each time his tail made contact, Gordon tightened his hand around Alasdair's neck, and Alasdair curled his talons into Gordon's chest. They were getting nowhere.

Alasdair slammed his free foot into Gordon's stomach with enough force that it caused his brother to loosen his hold. He then got his other arm between Gordon's limb and himself, further slackening the grip. It was enough for Alasdair to shove Gordon's arm to the side and break free.

He raked his talons down Gordon's chest, slicing through scales as blood bubbled between them, obscuring the water. When Gordon reached for him again, Alasdair was ready. He dodged to the side and twisted downward. Extending a wing, he slammed it into Gordon's face before swimming up behind him. The action bent his brother's tail at an odd angle and caused him to roar in fury.

Alasdair's tail whipped out to lash his brother's stomach when it struck the bottom of the loch. He waited until his feet touched, and then Alasdair pushed off, using a combination of strength and magic to get to the surface.

* * * *

Lotti ignored the soaked material that stuck to her skin and the dirt and debris that clung to it. She reached for Jeyra but wasn't sure where to touch her friend. Jeyra had so many cuts and abrasions that she looked ready to fall over.

"What happened?" Lotti asked.

Tears spilled from Jeyra's eyes, the look in them filled with fury. "They have him. They have Varek."

"Who?" But Lotti knew the answer.

Villette.

Jeyra swallowed, her arms clutched around the stone she held against her stomach.

"Was it Villette?" Lotti pushed.

Jeyra nodded. "And the Orgateans."

Lotti looked down at the stone and then at the water. Where was Alasdair? She should get into the lake and help him, but she couldn't leave Jeyra. Lotti swallowed hard and briefly squeezed her eyes closed before focusing on Jeyra. What if Villette caught Alasdair, too? She might be willing to trade one King for the stone, but Lotti doubted she would hand over both. That would mean a second trade. And there was one thing Villette wanted. Her.

After everything they had gone through to find the massirine stone, they would now have to trade it for Varek. She wished there was another option, but there wasn't. It was bad enough that Merrill was at Stonemore, even if he *did* remain by choice. Villette couldn't have her hands on two Dragon Kings. Not to mention, Jeyra needed her mate.

"Where's Alasdair?" Jeyra asked as if only just realizing he wasn't there.

Lotti opened her mouth to answer when Alasdair and Gordon launched from the water, gaining their attention. She watched in horror as the two of them crashed back into the lake with such force that it sounded like an explosion.

Lotti jumped to her feet, Jeyra forgotten, and ran to the shoreline. She struggled to see which of the two amethyst dragons was Alasdair as they thrashed around, half in the water and half out. Wings snapped, tails smacked against scales and water, and deafening roars filled the air. She winced at the sound of talons raking over hard scales.

Lotti was able to determine that Alasdair had a hold of Gordon. She knew the minute Gordon spotted her. He stopped struggling against Alasdair and kept himself facing her instead. And she knew why when he sucked in a breath. She saw his scales expand with his lungs, and then she saw the spark of flames.

She knew what was coming. Behind her, Jeyra screamed her name. Lotti waited until the first blast of dragon fire exploded from Gordon before imagining herself on the opposite side of the lake. She was gone before the fire reached her.

Lotti didn't take her eyes off the dragons. Gordon clawed up Alasdair's arms and face, anything he could reach. At one point, Gordon got a hold of Alasdair's wing and ripped it. She winced at the sound, knowing the pain must be intense, but Alasdair was focused. It was a brutal fight between two fierce dragons. Lotti waited for her chance. It came when Gordon succeeded in getting free.

He spun, sending a spray of water into the air in an arc, at the same time Alasdair attacked. She saw it all in slow motion. The water, Gordon's claws, Alasdair's bared teeth. Gordon was quicker. She pulled back her hand before shoving it outward with a shout of anger. The magic slammed into Gordon's side and knocked him backward. Lotti waited with another round of magic for when he turned to her, but he didn't budge. He simply floated, unmoving. But he wasn't dead.

She took a step into the lake. If he were left alive, he would come after Alasdair again. Lotti could prevent that. She used both hands this time, but he sank beneath the surface before she could deliver the killing blow. Lotti hurriedly walked into the lake, intending to go after Gordon.

Alasdair moved in front of her. He shook his dragon head, his jade eyes holding hers. She fought against a wave of panic when she saw the severity of his wounds, but they healed before her eyes.

"Jeyra," Lotti said, looking past Alasdair to where the warrior remained near the forest.

Lotti teleported beside her. Behind her, she heard the splash of moving water. When she looked, Alasdair had returned to his human form and was clothed and striding toward them.

He knelt on Jeyra's other side and briefly met Lotti's gaze before asking, "What happened?"

"We were attacked," Jeyra answered.

A muscle ticked in his jaw. "Villette?"

"And the Orgateans," Lotti added.

Jeyra drew in a shuddering breath. "They were waiting for us. They used some type of net. It nearly got me. He...I..."

Lotti covered Jeyra's hand with hers. She understood Jeyra's trepidation because she had experienced it herself. "Go on."

"I leaned away from the second net right when Varek dipped his wing to turn."

Alasdair briefly closed his eyes. "You lost your balance."

Fresh tears rolled down Jeyra's face. "I fell. Varek could've gotten away, but he swung around for me."

"You're his mate. He wouldna let anything happen to you," Alasdair said.

Jeyra's face creased in anguish. "They used that opportunity to cover him in nets. Still, he tried to get me somewhere safe. He had no choice but to drop me, or they would've taken me with him."

"The fall did this to you?" Lotti asked.

Jeyra nodded. "Aye. My people are in the forest. I ran here as fast as I could, but they're out there waiting."

Alasdair ran a hand down his face, his gaze locked on the stone. He lifted his eyes to Jeyra. "Villette will offer a trade—Varek for the stone."

"How do you know?" Jeyra asked.

Alasdair shrugged one shoulder. "It's what I would do. They wanted to get both you and Varek with the stone. They know what we've done to get to Merrill, and they expect the same for Varek."

"What are we going to do?" Jeyra's eyes were locked on Alasdair.

He nodded firmly. "We're going to get Varek back."

"That means Villette will have the massirine stone again," Lotti stated. "There has to be a way to keep it from her *and* get Varek."

Alasdair grinned as he got to his feet. "I never said we would give Villette the stone."

Chapter Twelve

Alasdair hadn't been this incensed since the war with the mortals on Earth. But now, that wrath was leveled on one individual: Villette. The overwhelming compulsion to engulf her in dragon fire and cause her more pain than she could possibly imagine was almost too much to set aside. If he gave in, he wouldn't stop. He would happily ensure Villette suffered for eons.

The list of her crimes was extensive and continued to multiply. She would be brought down. Alasdair was sure of that. The problem was that he couldn't guarantee when. He'd love to be the one who did it, but he knew it would take all the Dragon Kings and any allies they could gather. It wasn't time to end her rule. But they could hurt her.

He looked to his left where Jeyra stood. Her wounds were healing, though slowly. Lotti repaired Jeyra's clothing with magic. The warrior tried to refuse, but he warned her that Varek would lose his mind if he saw her in her current condition. Jeyra seemed to realize the truth of his words.

No doubt Varek was racked with guilt for having to release Jeyra. The last thing he needed was to see how much harm had come to her. But Jeyra was a fighter. The fact that she had held on to the stone despite the fall said a lot about her. Alasdair had always known she was tough, but he'd learned just how strong firsthand.

Alasdair swung his gaze to his right, where Lotti walked resolutely. She had wanted to go after Gordon, and while he agreed that his brother needed to be dealt with, they had to get Varek back first. Because Villette couldn't get her hands on any more Dragon Kings.

Maybe Alasdair should've gone after Gordon while Lotti and Jeyra went to locate Varek. Lotti's powers were evolving rapidly. He'd felt the ripples of the magic she'd used on Gordon. It was impressive and utterly devastating. No wonder it had knocked the dragon out. It would've been easy to end his brother's life then, but that wasn't Alasdair's way. He wanted Gordon conscious when he delivered the final blow. Just as he had when he fought him for the right to be King of Amethysts.

Then Gordon sank beneath the water, but not before he looked squarely at Alasdair, a promise in his citrine eyes. When they met again, only one of them would walk away.

"The Orgateans will be waiting," Jeyra said into the silence.

Alasdair fisted his hands at the reminder of yet more enemies they had to contend with. "I'm counting on it."

"Is that wise?"

He met Jeyra's amber eyes. "They have some kind of agreement with Stonemore. They'll be the ones to take us to Villette. Besides, any of the Orgateans with red hair can touch the stone like you."

Lotti asked, "Then what do we do? Walk straight up to them and announce we're trading for Varek?"

"Aye. Then double-cross them," he replied. There was a moment of silence as the women digested that.

"I take it you have something in mind," Lotti said with a grin.

Jeyra shook her head. "We don't know what will happen to Varek if we try something like that. We have to hand the stone to Villette for him to be returned."

"She won't willingly hand Varek over for anything. Not even the stone. She'll make sure she has it as well as Varek—and all of us," Lotti added.

Alasdair nodded, his lips pressing together. "That would be my plan. Varek knows Villette can no' be allowed to get her hands on the massirine again. He'll expect us to come up with a way to keep the stone *and* free him."

"I just want him back," Jeyra said, her soft voice filled with concern.

Lotti put her hand on a fallen tree to vault over the trunk. "We'll get him free."

"Aye." It was all Alasdair could muster. His rage remained too close to the surface each time he thought about Varek trapped with Villette.

"Should we have any other Kings join us?" Lotti asked. "It would give us an advantage."

"It would also start a war." Jeyra lifted her leg high and stepped onto the tree trunk before jumping to the ground on the other side.

Alasdair followed suit. "We're the ones who came for the stone, and we'll be the ones to fix this fuckery."

"What about Con? Should we alert him about what's going on? Or

Eurwen and Brandr?" Jeyra asked.

Alasdair grunted. "I've no' been able to reach any Kings. Let's hope I can call for aid if the time comes when it's needed."

"By then, they may have all of us," Jeyra replied.

Lotti cut her gaze to Jeyra before looking at Alasdair. "I'm going to make sure that doesn't happen. Villette has no idea what I can do now. She won't want to go up against me in front of everyone in case I best her."

"I agree. But doona underestimate her," Alasdair cautioned.

Lotti grinned. "She's the one who should be reminded of that about me."

"So, what's our plan?" Jeyra asked.

"Villette will anticipate a double-cross," Lotti added. "We need to take that into account."

Alasdair was about to reply when his enhanced hearing picked up the scraping sound of a sword being pulled from a scabbard. He halted. Lotti and Jeyra immediately did the same. He scanned the forest ahead.

Jeyra moved closer as she glanced behind her. "What is it?"

"We have company," he said in a low voice.

Jeyra's eyes narrowed. "The Orgateans."

Lotti's head swiveled as she studied her surroundings. "How close?"

"They're still some distance ahead," Alasdair answered. "My guess is they're lying in wait to ambush us. They'll surround us, then take us to Villette."

Lotti rolled her eyes. "Why do so many willingly want to fight a Dragon King? They have to know it means certain death."

"We're the enemy," Alasdair reminded her. "They only care about ridding the world of us."

Jeyra snorted. "This world started with the dragons."

"I don't think anyone cares about whose home it was," Lotti said.

Alasdair shook his head. "Trust me, they doona." He caught Jeyra's gaze. "You know your people. They despise dragons, especially the Kings. They'll take a chance to attack me."

Jeyra's lips twisted ruefully. "Sadly, you're right."

"Good. I want that." Alasdair smiled in response to Lotti's frown. "When it happens, you two stay together. It's what Villette will expect."

"Because I don't have magic and cannot fight as you two can. I agree. It makes sense for Lotti and me to team up," Jeyra said without heat.

Lotti nodded and looked at Alasdair. "They'll separate us from you."

"And we're going to make it easy for them to do exactly that," he said.

Jeyra shifted the large stone in her arms. "Why?"

Alasdair drew in a deep breath and slowly released it. "I want nothing more than to barrel through the Orgateans and Stonemore's soldiers. I'd love to crash into the city itself and grab Merrill and Varek. But I willna. Mainly because that's what Villette wants me to do. She's pushing us to the point where we let rage rule us. And we're much closer than she knows." He paused and slid his gaze to Lotti. "I'm no' the only one she's pushing either."

"What she's doing is wrong," Lotti said between clenched teeth.

Alasdair shot her a quick smile. "That's why we have to go about things strategically. We're no' going to attack the Orgateans. I willna even strike back when they launch their assault. Neither will either of you."

"And how is that going to get us the trade?" Jeyra questioned.

"I've been thinking about this since we left the lake. My gut tells me Villette will meet us outside of Stonemore. She doesna want Merrill to see any of this—or the people, for that matter. The Orgateans will bring us to her."

Lotti rolled her eyes. "After roughing us up, no doubt."

"No doubt," he said in agreement. "She'll probably put on some show. We'll talk."

Jeyra's frown deepened. "And Varek? Will we be able to see him?"

"That could go either way. She might have him somewhere he can see us. Just to bring home what's at stake." Alasdair shrugged. "That doesna matter because it's all for nothing. She willna trade for Varek, and we're no' going to give her the stone. She knows that the same way we do."

Lotti crossed her arms over her chest. "Which comes to Villette's double-cross. We saw how much the massirine stone means to her. But the thought of having three Kings as well as the stone in her control will be too much for her to resist."

"If you're right, Alasdair, we're going to be surrounded. How do we get out of the double-cross with the stone and Varek without starting a war?" Jeyra asked.

He smiled at Lotti. "You're the secret weapon."

For the first time, Jeyra's lips tilted in a semblance of a grin. "That's true. Yet all of this hinges on Villette being there. What if she sends someone in her place?"

"She'll be there," Lotti said.

Alasdair smiled as he put his hands on his hips. "Aye. I've no doubt she'll be the Divine's emissary. She willna let anyone else make decisions. And we're the only ones who know who she truly is."

"We could tell everyone," Jeyra suggested.

Lotti swatted at a bug flying around her face. "It wouldn't do any good. No one would believe us."

"Then how do we double-cross her?" Jeyra asked. "I get it's Lotti, but how?"

Alasdair blew out a breath before facing his mate. He didn't want to put undue pressure on her, especially since the plan would rely heavily on her powers. "I have an idea."

She raised her brows in response. "Go on. I'm listening."

Alasdair turned to Jeyra. "Hold out the stone, please." Once she did, Alasdair drew on his magic and created a replica in his hands, down to the tiny chip on the side.

"It looks just like it," Jeyra said. "But will Villette believe it is?"

Lotti twisted her lips. "She'll most likely want someone who has used it before to test it to see if they're able to look at the dragons through it."

"Then we ensure they see whatever they need to see," Alasdair said.

Lotti's eyes brightened with understanding. "I can make that happen."

"What do we do with this one?" Jeyra asked as she hugged the stone to her chest once more.

Alasdair met Lotti's turquoise gaze. "Can you teleport Jeyra to Iron Hall?"

Lotti hesitated. He knew she was considering her earlier attempt that had failed. They hadn't been in dire need then, not like they were now.

"Even if Lotti can get me to Iron Hall so I can drop off the stone, I'm returning. Besides, what if the replica doesn't work? What do we do then? We'll have nothing to trade for Varek," Jeyra stated.

Alasdair dropped his arms to his sides. "Then we fight."

"And begin the war everyone has been so desperate to avoid," Lotti said.

Alasdair threw up his hands. "We have no other option. Do we turn over the stone and expect Villette to willingly hand over Varek? We all know she's no' going to do that."

"We could take the stone out of the equation."

Jeyra's eyes widened at Lotti's suggestion. "We could do *what?*"

"I doona think that's an option, as much as I wish it could be. We need the stone to trade," Alasdair said.

Lotti shrugged a shoulder. "What if we make Villette think the stone was destroyed? It's a long shot, but if she believes the stone is out of her reach, she might give up on it."

"Doubtful," Alasdair said.

Jeyra shifted her feet nervously. "You said Villette will expect us to try and double-cross her. She'll never believe the stone is gone."

"Nay, I suppose not," Lotti said, her expression crestfallen. "I'm not keen on taking the real stone anywhere near Villette."

"I do have another idea, though," Alasdair said.

* * * *

"This had better work," Lotti whispered as they drew closer to the warriors lying in wait.

Jeyra grunted, her gaze sweeping the area.

Alasdair's entire body vibrated with awareness. He stopped and faced the girls. It was time to put their plan into motion. He looked at Jeyra. "Is this where you were when Varek dropped you?"

"Aye," she replied, shifting the replica stone in her arms. She jerked her chin to the left. "We were attacked from that direction."

Before they could move, the famed fighters from Orgate poured out from behind trees and bushes, shouting as they surrounded the trio. Jeyra's anger was real as she glared at her kinsmen. Lotti eyed them with distaste as blades moved near her face.

As for Alasdair, they gave him a wider berth when he turned to face them, but there was no denying their loathing. The feeling was mutual, but he didn't bother pointing that out. After all, the leader of Orgate, Arn, had trapped dragons and tortured them for years while siphoning their magic. Varek and Jeyra had discovered the atrocity and set things right—with the help of Death herself—Erith—and her Reapers.

The Orgateans wanted someone to blame. They put most of their focus on Jeyra, but the rest lay squarely with the Dragon Kings. Never mind what one of their own had done. It was the outsiders who would pay the price.

A tall, barrel-chested man with bushy, dark red hair and a long beard shouldered his way through the circle of warriors. He stopped at the edge of the circle and looked pointedly at Alasdair. "I have waited for this day for a long time. The beginning of the end of dragons has arrived. For all we've heard regarding how intelligent your kind is, you walked right into our trap."

Leave it to those with the biggest egos to convey important

information when they think they have already won. This might be easier than Alasdair had first thought. "You think you can hold me?"

The man grinned. "We've held plenty of dragons."

The hit came at Alasdair from behind. Pain exploded in his head. His knees buckled, and then blows began raining down.

Chapter Thirteen

Lotti shifted closer to Jeyra. She doubted anyone saw it, but it was just enough that when the warriors circled Alasdair, she and Jeyra were clumped together. So far, their plan was working. Then again, it had only just begun. There were too many players for things to go perfectly.

Lotti glanced at Jeyra. The warrior glared at a man who eyed her as if he wanted to cut her to pieces. The Orgateans celebrated their capture so loudly that Lotti could barely hear herself think. She had lost sight of Alasdair. Her heart thumped wildly against her ribs, and her palms dampened. So much rested on her. What if she failed? They would all be trapped.

"You can do this," Jeyra whispered, leaning close.

Lotti drew in a shaky breath. Her friends believed in her. Maybe it was time she had faith in herself. She nodded at Jeyra and tried to hear what the leader said to Alasdair, but Lotti couldn't make it out. She stiffened when she heard jeers and grunts.

"Don't," Jeyra warned. "Alasdair can handle whatever they dole out."

Lotti hated not knowing what was happening to him. With every groan and sound of pain, she knew Alasdair was being hit. He could end it. *She* could end it. But that wasn't the plan. Which made standing there looking helpless that much more difficult.

Her attention got yanked away when someone pulled her hands before her. Lotti bit back a wince. Her eyes widened when she saw the manacles. She cast a harried look at Jeyra, who was left unshackled. They had known encountering the chains that took away a Dragon King's power was possible. However, none of them knew if they would obstruct her magic as they did for the Kings. Lotti swallowed hard when the first click sounded as the cuff locked into place on her wrist. Fear froze her, and she stared at Jeyra as the second was about to latch. Then, it was too late to worry if the plans they had painstakingly put into action would be foiled.

Blood roared in Lotti's ears. She blinked several times to make sure she was seeing things correctly. She nearly laughed out loud when the fake stone remained visible, and the pack on Jeyra's back stayed hidden. The chains didn't hinder her power, and that meant she could get free anytime she wanted.

Suddenly, their captors shoved at her and Jeyra. Lotti stumbled, her shoulder hitting a tree before she found her balance, and they moved through the woods. Lotti tried to peer between the crush of bodies to glimpse Alasdair but was unsuccessful. The Orgateans kept their weapons drawn and pointed at her and Jeyra. Many of the blades came close to nicking them. It unnerved Lotti, but Jeyra ignored them. So, she tried to do the same.

The crowd trampled everything in their wake as they hiked through the forest, uncaring about damaging the habitat they disturbed. After all, they had seized a Dragon King and two women. In their eyes, they had won. Jeyra was intelligent and shrewd. Lotti expected the same from the other warriors from Orgate, but that wasn't what she had seen so far. These fighters actually thought they were good enough to catch them. It didn't appear as if any of them had any doubts they had triumphed. Lotti should be happy that the fools were so easily duped. If they weren't, their plan would have failed before it began.

She winced as the tip of a sword pressed into her back when she didn't walk fast enough. She threw a glower over her shoulder at the woman who had nudged her so callously. As she faced forward again, her eyes briefly met Jeyra's. They didn't talk as they walked beside each other, headed toward the Tunris Mountains.

They walked for hours, each step bringing them closer and closer to Villette. When the army came upon a steep slope down, Lotti took a moment to look ahead. It seemed most of the Orgateans were behind and to their side. A large group of warriors walked ahead and to the right of her, grouped around someone. She caught a glimpse of auburn hair just as they pushed Alasdair down the hill. Anger burned hotly in her veins when they laughed as he tumbled before slamming into a tree, halting his progress.

She didn't understand why Alasdair hadn't used his hands to right himself. Then she spotted the restraints. The same ones placed on her. The same special chains used on Varek to hinder his magic. Alasdair had expected such a tactic, but that didn't make it any easier to witness.

"Go," came a growl from behind before she felt another painful nudge.

Lotti and Jeyra exchanged glances. By Jeyra's frown, she had also seen the shackles on Alasdair's wrists. More pressure rested on Lotti. It had been one thing to hope and expect Alasdair to aid her if something went wrong, but now that wasn't possible. Everything rested on her.

She shifted sideways and began carefully making the descent. Lotti noticed that many around her eyed the large stone Jeyra held. Why had none tried to take it? They certainly had the numbers for it, and with Alasdair chained, it seemed the perfect opportunity. There was only one reason they hadn't. Villette.

Sweat ran down Lotti's back despite the cool autumn air. She doubted the warriors knew she was one of the Star People. Villette wouldn't disclose that there was someone so powerful within their midst. If she did, the Orgateans likely wouldn't have joined Stonemore's soldiers on this endeavor, and Villette needed the numbers. The more people around to witness two Dragon Kings' capture and the might and power of the Divine, the better.

Lotti discreetly looked around her. It was more than Villette not sharing information about the Star People. Villette thought her weak and incapable of tapping into the vast power of their kind. This was a test. One Villette expected Lotti to fail. The fact that she held Varek and intended to regain the stone was just a bonus. Because if everything went as Villette planned, the Divine's supremacy would be all but ensured.

That couldn't happen.

The pressure on Lotti multiplied. There wasn't an ounce of room for her to falter. She had to be on top of her game—one she had only recently begun playing. She had years to catch up on in a matter of minutes. No one would be there to pick up the slack or save the day. It was all on her.

The longer they traveled, the clamor of the Orgatean warriors eventually diminished to nothing. They didn't stop, didn't rest. The closer they got to the mountains, the more panicky Lotti became. She lost track of time as she envisioned the plan in her head, going over it again and again. She wanted to be ready when the time came so she didn't hesitate to use her magic. She imagined the projected outcome she wanted over and over as if it had already happened.

She was so engrossed in her thoughts that she ran into the back of the Orgatean in front of her when he halted. He muttered something unintelligible and gave her a nasty look. Lotti backed up a step to see that everyone had stopped. Her head swiveled to Jeyra, whose face was taut. Lotti didn't have to be told that it was time.

A wave of ice ran through her body. Her heart dropped to her feet, and her knees threatened to buckle beneath the weight of what was at stake. She searched the sea of warriors for Alasdair and somehow found him through the bodies to her right. His gaze was locked on her. She inwardly cursed when he gave her a barely perceptible shake of his head, letting her know he hadn't been able to reach Varek or any other King. They truly were on their own.

Suddenly, the soldiers grabbed Lotti and Jeyra by their upper arms and yanked them forward. The warriors parted, halfway turning to eye them with disdain. The fingers wrapped around Lotti's arm bit painfully into her flesh, but dread kept her from lashing out.

Jeyra, on the other hand, didn't hesitate to kick, her foot landing on the knee of the man who held her. The leg bent at an awkward angle, and he released her with a scream of pain, dropping to the ground to grab hold of his injured leg. This time, two men came up on either side of Jeyra and gripped her roughly. They yanked her so hard that she lost her footing and was dragged a ways before getting her feet beneath her again.

"I'm going to kill both of you," she declared through clenched teeth.

The men snickered, but it wasn't the raucous laugh from before. It was low and nearly inaudible. They knew exactly what Jeyra was capable of. Lotti took another look at the Orgateans. That was when she spotted it. Fear. Not for her or even Alasdair. Nay, it was all for Jeyra.

With Jeyra hauled ahead of her, Lotti got a good look at where they were. She bit back a grimace when she saw the mountain rising before them. They didn't take her there, though. It was to a rock that rose out of the ground to tower over them by ten feet. It had a flat surface with a shelf that extended over them. Lotti didn't take her eyes off it as they drew closer. A moment later, Villette walked out to stand above them.

Her blue gaze landed briefly on Lotti before moving to Jeyra and then finally Alasdair. Villette looked over the Orgateans as Stonemore soldiers dotted the hills and boulders behind her. Her long, blond hair was down and carefully combed to hide the right side of her face and neck. Lotti had seen the burns. She wasn't sure why Villette hadn't used magic to heal them, but she would find out. There was a reason, and they might be able to use it against her.

Villette clasped her hands before her and didn't bother to hide her satisfied smirk. Lotti wanted to slap it off her face. The fear that had ridden her hard on the way here was giving way to resentment. And rage.

"Don't let her get under your skin," Jeyra cautioned under her breath.

It was too late for that. Villette had to be stopped. Since the rest of the Star People had no interest in ending her reign of terror, Lotti would.

"I'm here at the behest of the Divine," Villette stated to the crowd. She swept her arm to the side. "We have captured a Dragon King. The Divine has promised that no dragons would harm Stonemore or any of our allies. The proof of the Divine's dominance is right before you."

The crowd cheered as a group of warriors pulled Varek into view. Jeyra stiffened, her body shaking with fury. He was covered with nets held down by at least three dozen Stonemore soldiers. He couldn't lift his head or stand straight. He roared loudly. Lotti saw a spark in his mouth and knew he wanted to release a round of fire, but he held back. Just so he wasn't the one to start the war.

Everyone needed to realize that it was inevitable. They should just accept that it had begun and act accordingly. But Lotti knew the Kings wouldn't do that. They were desperate to keep it at bay. So far, it had worked.

Villette's smile widened as she lowered her gaze to Lotti and clasped her hands before her once more. "You have something that doesn't belong to you."

"And you're holding someone you have no right to," Lotti replied. She was proud her voice sounded strong and determined and didn't waver. "We came to make a trade. The stone for Varek."

Villette's blue eyes moved over the crowd, her smile never faltering. "You dare to offer an exchange when we have you surrounded? You have no authority here."

Lotti felt Jeyra's shoulder brush against hers, a brief contact of support. She held Villette's gaze. "You know as well as I that more dragons will come if you continue to detain us. Or harm any of us. What nets you have won't be a match for the sheer numbers that will descend upon Stonemore. And its allies," she added, wanting to include Orgate in her threat.

This time, Villette's gaze skewered Jeyra. "What a pretty tattoo you have on your left arm. A dragon eye. There is meaning in that, I know."

A low, warning growl came from Varek.

It only caused Villette's smile to widen and her eyes to narrow into dangerous slits. Lotti grabbed Jeyra's hand. This was it.

"The Divine doesn't tolerate stealing. You came into our home and took what didn't belong to you," Villette announced in a loud, clear voice.

A murmur rose behind Lotti, but she kept her focus on her nemesis.

Timing was everything.

"You crossed our land, fought our soldiers, and…" Villette suddenly stopped, her gaze moving into the distance behind Lotti.

The first scream sounded. The next thing Lotti knew, people were tossed into the air.

Chapter Fourteen

Alasdair looked over his shoulder when he heard the commotion. Warning shouts mixed with those of shock and surprise. Then complete chaos erupted. Bodies flew all around him before landing with bone-crushing force. Stonemore soldiers stood frozen with fear while Orgatean warriors rushed about disorderly.

Unease ran like ice down Alasdair's spine. He heard someone ask if it was dragons. He knew it wasn't because that attack would come from the air. His gaze sought Lotti as he yanked at the shackles hindering him. He'd shift and get to Varek if he could, but the Orgateans had made sure that wasn't possible. The warriors guarding him no longer paid him any attention. Their focus was on whatever attacked from the rear.

Alasdair raced to Lotti, weaving around dead bodies and dodging warriors running either toward the fight or away from it. He caught the slightest hint of movement out of the corner of his eye before something hit him—like a battering ram driving into him. He heard ribs snap and felt bone pierce his lungs as the impact launched him to the side.

He should've been able to get to his feet, and his body should've begun healing instantly. But neither happened. He fought to stay conscious, even as it seemed some force was pushing him down, suffocating him. He knew in an instant that it was their invisible foe. Alasdair had to get to Lotti and Jeyra so they could break Varek free. But he couldn't even roll to his hands and knees.

Something weighty and malicious hovered over him. Alasdair tried to force his eyes open. A smell assaulted him, one he couldn't quite place. It took every ounce of strength he had to get his lids to obey, but there was nothing to see once he did. Still, he felt it. It was there, above him. Did it rejoice? Or was it waiting for him to make his next move?

Varek roared long and loud. Alasdair heard Lotti's voice over the pandemonium, shouting his name. He was able to turn his head enough to see her frantically searching for him. He didn't want her anywhere near the entity. There was no telling what it would do to her or Jeyra.

No sooner had the thought entered his mind than the cloying feeling vanished. His foe had turned its attention elsewhere, and Alasdair feared it was focused on Lotti. He let out a battle yell and forced himself to turn onto his side. He disregarded the dull ache of his slow-healing body and got his knees under him. Almost instantly, someone ran into him, knocking him to the ground again, their knee catching his still-healing ribs. He hissed in pain and tried to move quicker.

He couldn't remember ever being so…weak. And he despised it. The chains and the invisible foe wouldn't prevent him from getting to his mate. Alasdair gritted his teeth and bellowed his fury at his limitations, but he never stopped. He fought until he was finally on his feet. His gaze instantly went to Lotti. Jeyra watched her back as she cut the netting away from Varek.

Alasdair took a halting step toward Lotti. Then another. He caught a whiff of that familiar scent again, the one he couldn't place, and tried to move. But he wasn't fast enough. Breath rushed from him as he was struck twice in quick succession. Then a third. And a fourth.

* * * *

Lotti tossed aside the chains that had bound her and could only stare in shock at Alasdair being tossed around like a toy. Once he landed, she stared, silently willing him to move. She needed to get to him, but she couldn't leave until Varek was free.

"Nearly there," Jeyra said.

With one swipe, Lotti cut the remaining length of the net. Varek burst from the mesh and was almost instantly attacked. Jeyra cried out at the sight of her mate slamming backward into a boulder as if he were nothing but a fly.

"Get to him," Lotti told Jeyra.

Her friend glanced at her. "Are you coming?"

Lotti shook her head, her gaze locked on the one responsible for the mayhem. "Get Varek."

This was the invisible being that had attacked them before. She saw it clearly now. The floating entity was a knot of dark, swirling, angry energy with several tendrils trailing behind it like arms waving in the wind. There was no face, no body, but she sensed its pleasure in causing such confusion and pain.

The being moved fluidly and with such speed that it was difficult to track. Then, it suddenly stopped and faced her. At first, Lotti thought it was looking at her. Then she glanced over her shoulder to find Villette watching the carnage. Fear had frozen her. The thing didn't have a face, but Lotti felt its hatred as it started toward Villette.

Suddenly, the entity shifted its focus to a new target. To Lotti's horror, it was Jeyra and Varek. Lotti shouted their names, but the madness surrounding them drowned it out. Lotti raced toward her friends. The being dove between Varek and Jeyra, knocking them apart. It then spun around and went straight for the warrior, wrenching the fake massirine stone from her arms.

"Nay!" Villette screamed.

But it was too late. The entity had the stone. Lotti almost let it take it. Instead, she shattered Alasdair's replica. The entity paused before it turned its attention to Villette once more.

Lotti didn't care if the being got Villette. She focused on locating Alasdair. She grimaced when she found him in the same spot as before. Lotti motioned to Varek, who had pulled Jeyra to her feet. They had to get to Alasdair. "Hurry!"

She ran, shoving people out of her way and jumping over the ones on the ground. Lotti glanced at Villette, but she was gone. A quick look told her the entity was now locked on her and gaining ground quickly. She imagined being beside Alasdair with Jeyra and Varek with her. In the next instant, all three stood around him. Lotti barely had enough time to throw up her hands and create a domed shield around them before the entity struck.

"Fuck!" Varek bellowed.

Each time the being collided with her shield, it was like being hit herself. But Lotti would keep the shield in place for however long they needed it.

"Alasdair," she said and looked at him.

Varek knelt beside him. "He's out cold."

"It hit him four times." Lotti didn't think she would ever get the sight of seeing Alasdair flying through the air out of her mind.

Jeyra stared at her arms. She held them out in front of her as if they burned.

"Are you hurt?" Lotti asked.

The warrior shook her head, shaking free some strands of red hair that had come loose. "I don't think so. My skin just stings where it touched me."

"Did you see what it did to the stone?" Varek asked.

Lotti kept her hands up and magic flowing to the shield. "I destroyed the replica stone before it could take it."

Her words caused the entity to slam into the shield with more force. Lotti caught Jeyra's attention and motioned to Varek. The being could obviously hear them, and she didn't want it to learn their strategy. Lotti strengthened the shield as Jeyra whispered their plan to Varek.

Varek grunted when Jeyra finished. "Smart."

"What do we do now? We can't stay here," Jeyra said.

Varek straightened. "Lotti, you got us to Alasdair. Do you think you can teleport us to Iron Hall?"

"I can either keep up the shield or teleport. I can't do both." She hated that she wasn't powerful enough to get them away under cover. But she would be soon. She would make sure of it.

His lips twisted. "I was afraid of that."

"We have to make a run for it," Jeyra stated.

Lotti swallowed as the being struck, over and over. "It wants us."

"It could've killed me," Jeyra said. "Why didn't it?"

Varek shrugged. "I'm happy it didna."

"The way it attacked Alasdair makes me think it wanted to kill him. And it went after Villette," Lotti told them.

Varek's brows drew together. "How do you know?"

"I can see it."

Jeyra stilled, her eyes widening. "See it, see it? Not just where it's striking the shield?"

"Aye."

Varek held her gaze for a second before looking at Alasdair. "That could give us an advantage. The hits are sporadic. Can you see why?"

"It goes after others between its attacks on the shield. We'll have only moments when it backs off," Lotti said.

"We need to use the fact that it takes its attention off us. Otherwise, we'll never get out," Varek added.

Lotti knew they were right, but it didn't lessen her apprehension. Varek broke the shackles from Alasdair's wrists and tossed them aside. Then he draped Alasdair's body across his shoulders. Once Varek nodded that he was set, Lotti watched and waited as the entity returned to the shield and banged against it repeatedly.

With Villette gone, the soldiers and warriors ran around frantically. A few tried to search for the attacker, while many ran away. Lotti observed the being. It clearly enjoyed hurting others. The more pain it caused, the better. That warred with the knowledge that it wanted the four of them within the shield. It divided its attention in hopes of eventually getting to everyone. And it probably would if she didn't get them out.

"Get ready," Lotti said as the entity headed into a small contingent of soldiers seeing to the wounded.

As soon as it plowed through them, the being swung back to pummel her shield. Shouts drew its attention away. The second it turned, Lotti lowered the shield and said, "Move."

They started running. Even carrying Alasdair, Varek was ahead of them. Jeyra's long legs ate up the distance quicker than Lotti's. She knew when the being returned its attention to them. It was like being doused with a bucket of ice water.

Lotti thought about the forest and the ravine she and Jeyra had used. Then she thought about being there with Varek, Alasdair, and Jeyra, just as she felt a brush of air against her cheek from the entity. Fear clouded her mind, and her magic faltered. Lotti was so surprised when her power responded that she couldn't stop herself in time and tripped over a rock. Jeyra righted her with a nod and a smile.

"That was great timing," Varek said.

Lotti didn't look at him. Her attention was on Alasdair, who still hadn't woken. Varek laid him down, and Lotti was finally able to touch him. She smoothed a hand over her mate's face, silently urging him to wake. Raking her gaze over his body, she didn't see any blood, but that didn't mean he wasn't injured.

"He should be healed and awake. Why isn't he?" Lotti asked.

Varek blew out a breath. "The invisible foe affects us in ways we're still trying to understand. Alasdair suffered many blows. It might take him some time to stir."

Lotti didn't like that. She remembered how Alasdair had once absorbed her magic. It had mixed with his and allowed him to do incredible things. What if she could help him past whatever damage the entity had done? She laid her hand on his chest and gently pushed some of her magic into him. He still didn't move. She sat back on her haunches, crushed.

"You took us a fair distance from the battle," Varek said as he stood atop a boulder to look around. "We shouldna remain here long, however."

Lotti started to reply when Alasdair's eyes opened and locked on her. Her relief was so great her eyes welled with tears. "Hi," she said.

"Hey," he answered with a grin. But that quickly turned into a frown as he looked past her. "Where are we?"

Varek jumped to the ground and squatted on Alasdair's other side. "Lotti teleported us to a gully."

"The invisible foe," Alasdair said as he sat up.

Varek's lips twisted. "Aye. I'm no' sure whether to be happy it interrupted Villette's display or pissed because it attacked."

"I'm going to go with glad it interrupted," Jeyra said. "Though I'm happy Lotti was there to shield us from it and get us away."

Alasdair's gaze swung to Lotti. "You saved the day again, lass."

Lotti sat back, able to breathe for the first time in hours now that he was awake. "I can see the being now."

"How?" Alasdair asked with a confused shake of his head.

She shrugged. "I don't know."

"I'm no' complaining," Varek interjected.

Alasdair shot him a look before focusing on her once more. "What does it look like?"

"It's a churning ball of dark, angry energy. It doesn't have a face or a body. There are no eyes to know where it's looking, but I can sense it. It has tendrils trailing behind it like long, spindly limbs waving in the wind. And it takes pleasure in causing pain."

"I felt that myself," Alasdair said.

Lotti studied his face. "You were struck multiple times. Are you hurt?"

"My wounds are healing, though slower than usual. I'm no' sure if it's because of those damned chains or the entity."

Varek wrinkled his nose. "Might be both. I wasna injured when I wore the shackles, so I can no' say for sure."

"Regardless, I'm good. Just sluggish. Let's get home before that thing finds us again," Alasdair stated.

Jeyra wiped her mouth after taking a drink from the stream. "I wholeheartedly agree with that statement."

"Aye," Varek added.

Lotti got to her feet and pulled Alasdair up beside her. Then she was in his arms. They held each other for a long moment. So many things could've gone wrong, but they were somehow still together and in one piece. Their adventure wasn't over yet, though.

Chapter Fifteen

Alasdair wasn't used to his body taking so long to heal. It was getting there, but the lingering pain concerned him. The other Kings who had tangled with the invisible foe had experienced the same symptoms. That didn't make him feel any better, however.

"Are you really all right?" Lotti asked as she leaned back, her turquoise eyes studying him.

"Aye, lass. I'm in one piece."

Her brow furrowed deeply. "The way it attacked…"

Alasdair drew her into his arms again, as much for his benefit as hers. It felt good to hold her again and feel her soft body against his. He didn't try to lessen her concern. Everyone should be worried. The entity could inflict significant damage on a Dragon King.

He heard Varek's voice in his head and opened the mental link, even as his gaze shifted to where the couple still stood in an embrace off to the side.

"*The truth, brother. Are you okay?*" Varek asked.

Alasdair swallowed. "*I will be. The others who've encountered that thing survived without mishap. I will, too.*"

"*They were no' flung about like a rag doll as you were.*"

"*I doona need reminding.*"

"*We need to deal with that thing.*"

"*First, we have to get to Iron Hall.*"

"*You should know the foe went after the stone Jeyra held. Lotti destroyed it. Villette saw all of it.*"

Alasdair raised a brow. "*We could be free and clear, then.*"

"*With the way the entity kept coming back for the four of us, I'm no' so sure.*"

"*Then we need to get back quickly.*"

Varek nodded and severed the link. He placed a kiss on Jeyra's forehead before sharing a quiet conversation with her. Alasdair loosened his hold on Lotti. She took a step back, her gaze running over him once more.

"I'm here, lass. I'm fine," he assured her.

She didn't look convinced, but she didn't argue the point either. If he had seen her attacked as he'd been, he would likely act the same—if not worse. He stretched his body, working out the kinks. He wondered if he would ever stop aching. They either needed to figure out how the foe was hurting them or take it out. Preferably both. But one thing at a time.

"What now?" Jeyra asked. "Do we hide and wait for the cover of darkness to fly back home?"

Varek raised his brows as he shrugged. "It's no' a terrible idea. Lotti could shield us."

Alasdair looked closely at his mate and noted the lines of strain around her mouth and eyes. Her color was also off. She looked ready to pass out. "Lotti has used significant magic today. It's drained her. I doona want to add more."

"I can do it. Besides, we shouldn't tarry," Lotti said.

Alasdair took her hand in his. He knew she would try, and she could probably accomplish it, but at what cost?

"There's no need. You got us here. And then there's the...thing. We can do the rest to get home," Jeyra said with a soft smile.

Varek nodded in agreement. "If we're going, then let's decide on a route and get moving before something finds us."

"It's a straight shot from here, but if anyone is looking for us, they'll likely wait along that route," Lotti said.

Alasdair ran a hand through his hair, shoving it away from his face. "If we can no' take to the skies, and we can no' head straight to Iron Hall, I suggest we go the long way around."

"Over the mountain? You want to be that close to Stonemore?" Varek asked, alarm tightening his face.

Lotti shook her head. "Going near Stonemore would be as big of a mistake as it would be to return through the forest. Villette wants Dragon Kings. The last thing we should do is put any of you near her."

"We're no' afraid of her," Alasdair said.

Lotti swung her gaze to him. "Maybe you should be. I don't like how far she's going with things. We stole the stone, and she used that to gather her armies. Soon, she won't need a reason. She'll come straight for you."

"Let her," Varek replied in a dangerously low tone. "I'll be happy to show her just what we think of her."

Jeyra slowly shook her head, her brow lined. "And what about

Merrill? Alasdair, I know you were able to speak to him briefly, and he decided to remain at Stonemore, but what if he isn't strong enough? What if she breaks him?"

"Never," Varek replied.

But Alasdair saw the unease in Varek's clenched jaw. He felt it, too. They should be pleased that they had someone on the inside with Villette, but no matter how Alasdair tried to look at it, he couldn't shake the ominous feeling.

"We can't do anything about Merrill now," Lotti pointed out. "We need to focus on getting ourselves home."

Alasdair looked to his left and then his right. "Maybe we should split up."

"I don't think so," Jeyra said.

At the same time, Lotti replied, "Nay."

Varek chuckled and looked at Alasdair. "I agree with the girls."

Alasdair faced the mountains. He could just make out the peaks through the trees. The one thing they could agree on was not staying in the area. Going the long way around would bring them near Stonemore on their trek to Iron Hall. The only way they could get home quickly was by flying.

"What do we know as fact?" Alasdair asked as he turned to the others.

Jeyra tilted her head. "Villette will keep coming for us."

"She doesna care when or where," Varek added.

Lotti tucked her hair behind an ear. "And she's scared of the entity."

"What else?" Alasdair prompted.

Lotti dropped her gaze to the ground for a moment. "The being isn't encumbered by a body. It floats and zips around so rapidly that it's difficult to keep track of it. It would be able to find us anywhere, at any time."

"Whether we're on the ground or flying," Varek said.

Jeyra shot a worried look at Varek. "It already killed too many dragons."

"No Kings, though," Alasdair pointed out. And he hoped it never did.

Varek rubbed his hands together. "We have two enemies to consider."

"And both are powerful," Lotti replied.

Jeyra's nose wrinkled in distaste. "I hate to say it, but Villette hasn't tried to kill a King yet. The entity has. We need to take that into account."

"Villette might not have sought to take a King's life, but she wants to capture as many of you as she can," Lotti said.

Varek sighed and shifted, planting his feet wider. "Both are formidable."

"I doona no' relish fighting something I can no' see. Worse, doing it in the air thousands of feet aboveground," Alasdair said.

Lotti grinned. "I can shield us so we can't be seen. And I can see it."

"I doona want to overtax your powers. You've done a lot. You're still using them. No' to mention you would be shielding two dragons."

"I can attempt to teleport us to Iron Hall now."

Jeyra's eyes widened in excitement. "Do you think you can?"

"I won't know until I try."

It was the best alternative, but Alasdair couldn't shake his apprehension. It wasn't that he questioned Lotti's abilities. She came through in a clutch every time. But she would never forgive herself if she failed and someone were harmed.

"I can do this," she stated.

Alasdair slid his gaze to her to find her staring at him. She had spoken the words for his benefit. "Aye, lass. I know you can."

"Do you?" Her brows were raised in question.

He squeezed her hand. "Without a doubt. We're standing here now because of you."

"Then let me do this."

"I'm no' stopping you. I want us to get home as much as you do."

Her lips softened. "Then let's go home."

"Are you sure you want to do that?"

The four of them stiffened at the sound of Villette's voice. Alasdair looked up to find her standing on the hillside above them with her arms crossed. Her annoyance was clear in the way she had her blue gaze narrowed on them.

"Go," he whispered to Lotti. "Take Jeyra."

Villette laughed as she dropped her arms to her sides. "No one is going anywhere."

"I wouldna be so sure of that," Alasdair replied coolly.

Villette rolled her eyes. "You dragons think you're always in the right."

"Because we usually are," Varek quipped.

Lotti asked, "What do you want, Villette?"

"A beautiful sunset, Merrill naked in my bed, and, oh…aye, the utter domination of this realm and then the entire universe."

Alasdair barely held back his revulsion. "No' going to happen."

Villette shrugged one shoulder. "I've been planning for a long time. Nothing will stop me."

"Seems like something did. It took out your forces and made you run," Lotti said.

Villette quirked a brow as she smirked. "It also tossed dragons around like leaves on the wind. I took great enjoyment in that."

Alasdair's fury rose at an alarming rate. If they weren't afraid of the war Villette wanted, he'd throw caution to the wind, attack Stonemore, and rip the city apart. But that wasn't what really caused his indignation. Nay, that was reserved for Villette and the hatred and prejudice she advocated, the bigotry that had been allowed to run rampant through the city and spread like a virus across Zora. He could flatten the mountain and wipe out any mention of Zora. He could kill Villette. But none of it would stop the injustice and bias she had cultivated.

"I'll ask again," Lotti said. "What do you want?"

Villette's smile spread slowly. "All of you. You didn't actually think to get away from me, did you? After you stole from me?"

Alasdair said Varek's name through the mental link. To his shock, he heard him.

"We're fucked, brother," Varek said.

Alasdair wasn't going down that easily. *"It's four against one."*

"Until our unseeable foe returns."

"Are you with me?"

Varek snorted. *"As if you need to ask. Let's show this bitch what we really think of her."*

"Get ready." Alasdair reached out to Cullen. Villette liked to control things by preventing the Kings from communicating. The fact that Cullen answered worried Alasdair. He gave him a quick rundown so Cullen could be ready before returning his attention to Villette.

Lotti released his hand and took a step forward. She tilted her head to the side, and a small frown furrowed her brow. "You wish to go against the four of us?"

"My kind rules galaxies. I can handle two Dragon Kings, an Orgatean warrior, and one who has barely learned her powers," Villette sneered. "With ease."

Alasdair backed up slowly, putting distance between him and Lotti so he had enough room to shift. It would be extremely tight in the gully, but he didn't intend to stay long once he changed forms. "What are you waiting for, then?"

Villette drew in a quick breath and raised her head to look without answering. Alasdair exchanged looks with the other three. He picked up a distant sound. Then he felt the ground trembling beneath his feet. Villette's laugh only infuriated him as she stood on her perch above.

"I always get my revenge," Villette said, her voice rising over the growing noise. "This should get the being's attention. It'll finish you off."

Lotti's hands were fisted at her sides. "Coward."

Alasdair hastily looked around. He couldn't see what was coming from his position in the gulch. Jeyra had already slipped away to climb the embankment. Varek backed farther away.

"It's called being clever," Villette shouted above the racket.

The ground shook so severely that the trees shuddered and swayed, sending leaves that had clung desperately to branches raining down around them. Alasdair opened his mouth to call out a warning to Lotti when a huge beast leapt over the gully. He looked at the thick green skin similar to an elephant's and the two horns protruding from its head as the animal sailed over them before crashing into the side of the ravine and sliding down to the water. It shook its great head and swung around.

Alasdair had heard about the brinelings, but this was the first time he had seen one. He was shocked at how swiftly the beast moved for its size. Once the animal locked its eyes on them, it roared and charged, just as more of the brinelings fell around them.

Chapter Sixteen

Lotti shouted a warning, but no one heard her over the racket. She heard a tree splinter seconds before it fell and dropped onto one of the ferocious beasts. Within moments, over a dozen disoriented and angry brinelings were in the ravine with them. Lotti spotted Jeyra clinging to the slope as a brineling foot nearly hit her in the head as it plunged into the gully with a horrible scream.

Alasdair and Varek shifted. The two dragons, along with the brinelings, meant there was little room left in the chasm. Lotti turned in time to see one of the animals barreling toward her. She raised her hands to use protective magic, but before she could, the beast released a shriek when Alasdair flung the animal away with his tail.

Lotti stood at the ready to keep the brinelings at bay, but they had focused their attention on Alasdair and Varek. They were using a combination of strength and magic to alternately calm the beasts and send them away. Lotti backed toward the slope to stay out of the way. She looked toward Jeyra again to find the warrior had reached the top of the ravine and rolled onto solid ground.

As much as Lotti wanted to confront Villette, who was no doubt watching nearby, she kept her eyes peeled for the entity. Villette was calling it here. Lotti couldn't see much in her current location. She tried to teleport to the top near Jeyra. It was a short jump—and an easy one at that—but her power failed again.

She barely had time to duck as Varek spun, his tail and a wing nearly clipping her. She tried again to teleport to Jeyra. This time, it worked. Lotti turned in a circle, searching for the being and Villette. All she saw, however, was the carnage the stampede had left behind. The forest was eerily still, other than the battle below.

"I don't like this," Jeyra whispered, surveying the woods.

Lotti pressed her lips together as the hairs on the back of her neck rose. "Be on the lookout. We're not alone."

"Aye. I feel it, too."

Lotti slowly turned, her gaze moving up to the trees and then along the ground, searching for the entity. Instead, she found Villette on the opposite bank, a smirk on her face as she dared Lotti to come for her. And she fell for it. She had a chance to end Villette, and she was going to take it.

"You're finished here," Lotti declared after teleporting across the chasm to stand six feet from her enemy.

Villette smiled, chuckling. "Oh, ho. Bold words. Especially coming from a baby such as you."

"No more will you disrupt life on Zora. Whatever *plans* you had will never come to fruition." Lotti took a step closer. Anger pulsed through her for everything Villette had done—and would do if someone didn't put an end to her. "You won't be sending armies or Gordon or anyone else after me or my friends."

"You think to stop me?"

"Aye." The wind blew the hair away from Villette's face, giving Lotti a clear view of her burns.

There was a hint of respect in Villette's blue eyes as she returned Lotti's stare. "You know nothing about this world or any of the others out there, or how inconsequential other beings are compared to us. You have no idea what it feels like to soar among the stars. You can only guess at the power our kind has because you've barely touched upon it. You want to be the dragons' savior. I can see it on your face. You think you've found a place to belong but you haven't. There's only one place you're truly suited for, little sister, and that's with us. Your family." Villette shrugged nonchalantly. "Though none of us want you."

"Maybe you're the one they don't want." It was a guess, but the way Villette's eyes narrowed told Lotti that her words had struck a nerve. "Eurielle stood against you. The others aren't helping you achieve the domination you crave. I wonder why you want to rule such insignificant people on an unimportant realm when you could be out among the stars. Could it be because *you* don't have a place with our kind?"

Villette's face tightened with indignation. "I was going to let you live. I was willing to take you under my wing and show you the universe. But no more. I'll take everything you hold dear and destroy it all. Beginning with Alasdair. I will make you watch as he succumbs to a slow, violent death. You'll be helpless to do anything but watch as I kill dragon after dragon until every last one of their corpses is rotting on the ground. Then,

I'm going to Earth to finish off the Kings. By the time I'm finished, there won't be a dragon left in the entire universe."

A rush of fury sent fire running through Lotti's veins. Villette meant every word, and it would be up to Lotti to stop her. "You won't touch anyone on Zora or anywhere else."

"Such confidence for one who has never seen war. You stand before me with such righteous anger now, but it won't be long before you're on your knees begging me to stop."

Lotti's rage slowly cooled to stony resolve. It allowed her to see Villette for who she really was—a woman without a home or family. A woman without *anything*. "You control others with fear. When you need them—because you will—no one will be there for you."

"I don't need anyone. I never have."

"Just as no one will mourn you when you're gone."

Villette scoffed at her words. "You're about to find out just who you're playing with, little sister. You should be worried because I won't stop until you're dead."

Lotti knew the hit was coming. She anticipated it and spun to the side, but the blast of Villette's power still grazed her. The pain was agonizing. All she wanted to do was curl into herself to make it stop, but that meant certain death. Lotti clenched her jaw and retaliated. It was a pitiful display that barely pushed Villette back two inches.

She looked down at the ground and then up at Lotti before releasing a laugh. "This is going to be too easy."

Lotti ducked, turned, and rolled as Villette released burst after burst of magic so quickly Lotti had no time to strike back. A yelp escaped when one struck her in the shoulder and spun her around before another landed on her back, slamming her face-first into a tree, the bark biting into her cheek. Warm, wet liquid ran down her face and dropped against her lips. Lotti detected the distinctive coppery taste of blood.

Her anger was banked, and panic threatened to take hold. She pushed both away and sought the tranquility she had attained before their battle had begun. Lotti spun on her heel and dropped to one knee, throwing out both hands, palms forward. The force of the magic that left her rocked her. She righted herself just as her power slammed into Villette. She doubled over and flew backward from the punch of Lotti's magic.

Lotti climbed to her feet with determination. She lifted her hands for another round as Villette slowly rose to one elbow. Their gazes met. No longer did Villette look quite so confident.

"Lotti!" Jeyra screamed.

She looked toward Jeyra to find the warrior waving her hands and jumping up and down before pointing down into the ravine. Lotti's heart sank when she saw Varek and Alasdair lying unmoving and in their human forms. Lotti's eyes darted about until she spotted the entity.

Villette was forgotten the instant Lotti saw the entity's dark form headed straight for Alasdair. Out of the corner of her eye, she saw Jeyra jumping down to the slope and sliding to the bottom of the gully. One minute, Lotti was at the top of the gulch. The next, she found herself in the entity's path.

"Nay!" she screamed, holding up her hands to stop it.

The being reared back as if struck. It darted away, only to circle around to attack from another direction. Lotti was having none of it. She was closest to Alasdair and bent to grab his ankle before teleporting next to Jeyra and Varek. Lotti got the shield up before the entity reached them, but it was close. Closer than last time. The being had anticipated her move and reacted in kind.

It repeatedly banged furiously against the shield. There was no one else to take its attention off them, and that meant there was no relief for Lotti. She heard Jeyra calling Varek's name, but he had yet to answer. Lotti wanted to check on Alasdair, but she didn't dare take her attention off the shield or the entity for even a second. It took everything she had to keep the being out.

Alasdair had been right. She was exhausted. She wasn't used to expending her energy and using her powers the way she had today, and it had drained her to the point where she feared she had put them all in a dire predicament. If only she hadn't gone after Villette. Why had Lotti thought she could remove one of their enemies by herself? Villette wouldn't go down that easily, and Lotti wasn't strong enough to take her on alone. She had learned that the hard way. It was a lesson she wouldn't soon forget.

The ease in which Villette wrought her magic was something Lotti needed to learn. And fast. But first, they had to survive this attack from the entity. They had gotten away the first time, mostly due to luck. Lotti wasn't sure they could do it a second time.

She glanced at Jeyra, who finished checking on Alasdair. "How is he?" Lotti asked.

"As non-responsive as Varek. We need to get home. Can you get us there?"

Lotti shook her head, regret sitting sourly in her stomach. "I don't think so."

Jeyra's brief smile was tight and filled with trepidation. "We'll find another way."

Would they? Lotti closed her eyes against a wave of exhaustion. Her arms began to shake, the muscles overtaxed. She needed a minute to relax, but she couldn't afford to do that. The entity was looking for a weakness, and the instant she let her guard down, it would seize the opportunity. Her gaze lingered on her beloved. How many times had the being struck Alasdair? Would there be lasting damage? Would he wake?

If only she had kept her place as a lookout, she could've stopped him from being attacked again. But it was done. There was no use wishing to undo something that was in the past.

Lotti gritted her teeth and resumed her position when the entity struck the shield with such force that she stumbled back a step. She refocused on the being and put everything she had into keeping her shield up, but it was becoming more difficult by the minute. She felt it weakening with each strike. She repositioned her feet and pushed past the pain spreading through her.

The hairs on the back of her neck rose. Lotti turned her head to one side and then the other before finding Villette watching them. There was a brief break in the being slamming into the shield, as if it, too, had caught sight of her. Villette vanished before the entity could turn on her. Lotti lifted her chin in defiance as the being returned to its intent to break through the shield.

The problem? It was working. She could see tiny cracks everywhere.

She closed her eyes and focused on staying on her feet while keeping her magic strong. She faltered a few times, but somehow she kept going. The passage of time became irrelevant. Sooner or later, the entity had to tire of them. Eventually, it would give up. Surely. They would have seconds to get away, and she had to be ready for that. It was their only chance.

If she were stronger, she could teleport them back to Iron Hall. If she were able to harness her power better, she could keep the shield up *and* get them all to safety. So many variables. None of them mattered in this moment. For now, she had to keep the shield up. She had to protect her family.

Her knee buckled, and she went down hard, her trouser leg instantly soaked from the stream. She wished she could take a drink. She didn't know how much time had passed before her other knee gave out. Lotti opened her eyes to see that night had fallen. The entity now rammed the shield near her. There were so many fissures now she was surprised it remained intact.

Someone said her name. She thought it was Alasdair, but that was likely just her brain making her think it was him. She tried to get to her feet once more, but she had nothing left in her body. The being smacked the shield again. Her heart dropped to her stomach when she heard it crack.

Chapter Seventeen

Alarm churned through Alasdair when Lotti didn't respond to him calling her name. He held her upright, lending her his strength as hers waned. He glared at the part of the shield that vibrated each time the entity struck it. He might not be able to see their foe, but he knew where it was. Every hit seemed to weaken her, and there was nothing he could do. Behind him, Varek and Jeyra were poised for battle.

"Varek," he called.

"I'm trying," Varek answered. A moment later, he cursed. "My magic does nothing to stop that thing."

Alasdair added his magic to Varek's. "Doona stop!"

The magic of two Dragon Kings was doing nothing to stop the entity from getting through Lotti's shield. If only he had been awake to absorb some of Lotti's magic. Maybe they could've fought it together. But time was running out for them.

And there was only one way Alasdair knew they could fight it.

"Varek!" he shouted through their mental link. *"Let's fry this asshole."*

"Gladly," Varek replied.

"Wait until the shield collapses. We know where it'll be. Blast it with everything you have."

No sooner were the words out than the shield began to waver. They had seconds to prepare, but that was all Alasdair needed.

With the shield down, he shifted, catching Lotti in his hand at the same time he blew fire, engulfing the entity. They couldn't see the enemy, even with their enhanced vision, but the blaze perfectly outlined a round being the size of a beach ball and its wispy tendrils like remnants of tattered clothing. Alasdair inwardly grinned as their foe thrashed about in obvious pain. Then Varek's dragon fire joined his.

The entity dropped to the ground and rolled. Despite the evidence of their foe's anguish, it wasn't burning as it should. Alasdair inhaled and released another long breath. Varek did the same. And still, the entity lived.

They tried to keep it locked within their fire, but it was difficult with the way it spun and flopped in the water and over the boulders. Alasdair lost it and had to move until he found the bastard within Varek's flames. Then the entity shot straight upward. They followed with their fire, reaching as far as they could until the being was out of sight.

As much as Alasdair wanted to find it and finish it off, they had other pressing matters to attend to. Alasdair prepared to take flight as Jeyra settled on Varek's back. The night would help hide them, and if anyone *did* spot them, they would deal with it later. He needed to get Lotti somewhere safe so he could see to her. She hadn't stirred since falling unconscious, and that worried him.

Varek leapt into the air. He spread his wings to catch a current when Jeyra tumbled off him, briefly landing on his wing before she hit the ground. Alasdair turned to help when he realized she hadn't fallen. She'd been struck. The entity had returned. Varek swung his large body around, slamming into the side of the ravine and causing rocks and small trees to fall around them.

Jeyra was on her stomach as something ripped at the pack on her back. Lotti's magic no longer concealed the massirine stone. None of them had noticed that the illusion concealing it had been interrupted since their attention was on the shield. But now they had another fight on their hands.

Varek landed next to Jeyra, but neither he nor Alasdair could do anything. Jeyra was too near the entity for them to be able to blast it with fire again. They stood on either side of her, watching and waiting. She managed to slip out of the pack and roll to Varek. When she was safe with him, they once more engulfed the entity in fire.

Alasdair could've sworn he heard a howl of agony. He wanted this thing to hurt. He wanted it to suffer unimaginable pain. But more than anything, he wanted it dead. He and Varek wouldn't stop this time until it was.

They had it locked in place, standing on either side of it. Each time it moved, they shifted to keep it boxed in. At least he thought they did until the pack shriveled to nothing, and the stone started to melt. Then, the entity was just...gone. They hadn't been able to track it like last time. It could be dead. He didn't know what it was made of, but they weren't waiting around to find out if it was still alive.

Jeyra scrambled into Varek's hand, and then they were in the air.

Alasdair was right behind them. He opened his palm to glance at Lotti. She lay as still as death, the wind moving her hair. He closed his hand gently as they flew to Iron Hall as fast as they could. Alasdair kept waiting for another attack from the entity, but none came. Maybe the being was dead. Or perhaps they'd hurt it more than they realized.

Finally, he spotted Raynia Canyon. Cullen stood in the moonlight with Nari, waiting for them. Varek was the first to dive into the canyon. Alasdair remained in the sky among the few clouds until Varek returned to human form. Then he dove straight down, tucking his wings against his body. He spread them at the last minute to come to a halt, then flapped a few times until he landed softly and could shift. He didn't bother with clothes as he strode to the hidden door with Lotti in his arms.

Jeyra and Varek stood by the entrance, their faces lined with concern. Cullen came up beside him but remained silent. Alasdair was grateful. There would be time to talk later once his mate was awake. He walked inside and raced down the steps. Tamlyn came out of the kitchen holding Ben. On her heels was Sian in her alchemy apron and gloves with a container of something in her hand.

Alasdair didn't slow. He moved quickly through the corridors until he reached their chamber. Once inside the darkened room, he gently laid her on the bed, kissed her forehead, and lit the room with magic. Then he meticulously checked her for injuries. He straightened when he found her body free of wounds.

"My turn," Sian said without looking at him.

He glanced at the petite woman who moved to stand across the bed from him. It was on the tip of his tongue to tell her there was nothing she could do. Lotti wasn't human. What did Sian know about Star People? What did *any* of them know?

Not much. Which was the problem.

Varek and Cullen came up on either side of him. It was Cullen who said, "Let Sian have a look."

Alasdair nodded woodenly, the fear clamped around his heart tightening its hold.

Varek placed a hand on his shoulder. "Come, brother. Give her room."

"I'm no' leaving," Alasdair stated.

Sian opened one of Lotti's eyes and looked at her pupil. "Then put some clothes on."

Alasdair winced when he realized he was still naked. He called clothes to him, and when Varek urged him to leave a second time, he went with his brothers into the hall. He leaned back against a wall and dropped his chin to his chest.

"What the fuck happened?" Cullen asked.

Alasdair shook his head. "Which part?"

"I filled Cullen in on everything that happened from the time we parted at the lake," Varek said.

Alasdair lifted his head and ran a hand down his face. That had only happened hours earlier. It felt like days ago. Maybe even weeks. The last thing he wanted to do was talk, but his fellow Kings needed to know what they were up against. Besides, he had to do something to take his mind off Lotti.

After a long sigh, Alasdair shared with Varek and Cullen the events leading up to the last battle with Gordon. Varek jumped in and told them how he and Jeyra were attacked. Rage burned hotly through Alasdair when he heard how the netting was used on Varek. Then it was Alasdair's turn to share details about the trek he'd made with the girls to trade for Varek. From there, he and Varek took turns finishing the story until they arrived at the present in Iron Hall.

"Fuck," Cullen said, pivoting to take a few steps away before turning back. His hands were fisted at his sides. "Those bloody shackles. I'd hoped we'd seen the last of those, yet those infernal people used them again."

Alasdair grunted. "I've never had my magic hindered in such a way. It was…"

"Fucking horrible," Varek finished.

Alasdair looked at him and nodded.

"Now we also have to contend with the netting." Cullen shook his head, his nostrils flaring. "Shite."

Varek crossed his arms over his chest. "We're used to being the dominant species. At least on Earth, the humans didna try to trap us and obstruct our magic."

"They probably would've if they had been brainwashed as these people are," Alasdair said.

Cullen shook his head again. "We need to figure out how to impede the use of the chains. Same with the netting. I doona suppose either of you happened to bring a sample back with you as you did that metal arrow from Stonemore."

"That was the last thing I was thinking about," Alasdair said, glancing at the door.

Varek twisted his lips. "We had what we went for."

"It really melted?" Cullen asked with a frown.

Alasdair nodded slowly. "Aye. Too bad the entity didna go down with it."

"Are you sure it didna?" Cullen shrugged. "You didna see it fly away."

Varek scratched his jaw. "We can no' be sure either way."

They fell into silence, each thinking about the day. They should rejoice at having found the stone, as well as getting away from Villette, but it didn't feel like much of a victory with the stone melted, and Lotti unconscious.

Sian walked out of the chamber. She had her thick gloves tucked under one arm as she shoved a wavy lock of brunette hair that had fallen out of her bun away from her face. Her green eyes met his. "I didn't find any external injuries as you, yourself, saw. I don't think there is any internal damage either. It's hard to tell since I have nothing to compare her to. She looks human, and that's all I can go by. Her heart rate is normal, as is her breathing. It appears as if she's simply resting."

"I wager she's doing more than that," Varek said. "Especially after the amount of power she used."

"Is there nothing you can do?" Alasdair asked Sian.

She shook her head. "I've tended to many who have different types of magic, but I've never examined a Star Person. Like Varek said, she expended more energy than she ever has before. And Lotti is just coming into her power. It could be that she just needs time to restore herself, for lack of a better word. We wouldn't even notice something like this if she were a child. Because for one, she wouldn't have used so much, and two, she would be learning her magic as she advanced."

"And she's trying to do everything now," Alasdair added. He had pushed her.

Varek caught his gaze. "Doona think this is your fault."

"How can it no' be? I'm the one who came up with the plan for her to hide the stone and pack on Jeyra. There are also the encounters with Gordon, her skirmish with Villette, and the invisible foe. Let's no' forget that I was unconscious and had to be protected instead of helping."

Varek's face hardened. "Hold up there, brother. She was defending all of us. It wouldna have mattered if you were awake or no'."

"Varek's right," Cullen added. "Lotti did what she had to do in grim situations. We've all been there."

Sian slapped her gloves against her leg. "One thing. Lotti will probably blame herself for not being able to get everyone home when she wakes."

"It wasna her fault," Alasdair argued.

Cullen looked at him pointedly. "And neither is it yours. It's no one's."

"It was the situation. Which sucked. But we're home. All of us," Varek said.

Sian gave a nod. "That's what should be celebrated. There's no blame here."

Alasdair knew they were right. But he'd feel better about all of it once Lotti woke.

Chapter Eighteen

Alasdair refused to leave Lotti's side. When sitting became too tedious, he stood. When that grew tiring, he paced the chamber, only to repeat the process all over again. Minutes ticked by slowly, and with each one, his fear increased tenfold.

Sian visited every hour. She said little as she quickly examined Lotti before leaving once more. Varek and Jeyra came. They tried to talk to him, but he couldn't pull himself from his thoughts to take part in any conversation. Varek returned later, but this time, he said nothing. He just stood beside Alasdair to offer silent comfort.

Cullen visited nearly as often as Sian did. Sometimes, he poked his head in the door and left. Other times, he sat with Alasdair. Tamlyn came twice. Once alone, and another time with Ben. Without a word, she placed the bairn in Alasdair's arms and walked away. He'd been furious until he looked down and found the child looking up at him with wide eyes.

Alasdair was instantly transported to the day he had stumbled upon Lotti and the bairn. Babies were highly regarded on Zora because only animals and dragons could bear young. Yet someone brought bairns to the realm. No one knew how or why. Yet. Lotti had discovered the infant wailing. If it hadn't been for Ben, Lotti wouldn't have been in that location, and Alasdair would never have found his mate.

He pressed a kiss to the bairn's forehead and realized that holding him had eased Alasdair a little. He didn't know how long he held Ben before he drifted off to sleep. When Tamlyn came to retrieve Benneit for his feeding, Alasdair had a hard time handing him over. Ben would be raised with the other rescued children from Stonemore.

A part of Alasdair wanted to claim the child for his own, especially after what they had just been through. But it was precisely *because* of what he and Lotti had endured that Ben was better off with Cullen and Tamlyn.

Not that Cullen wouldn't jump into a battle when he was needed—and sometimes even when he wasn't. Cullen was a Dragon King, after all. But Cullen and Tamlyn had made a home for themselves in the underground city.

Alasdair leaned forward in his chair and braced his forearms on his thighs before dropping his chin to his chest. He knew Lotti was extremely powerful and a true immortal, if Erith was confirmed as a Star Person. But Star People could be killed. Just as everything could. Even Dragon Kings. He knew it was unreasonable to wish to prevent anything bad from happening to Lotti. Every being who loved knew what it was to fear losing someone. He was no different. Yet it *felt* different.

Lotti had more of a chance of living forever than he did, but he still wanted that extra layer of security by undergoing the mating ceremony. He told himself it was absurd, but a part of him was sure she would be safe if she bore the dragon eye mark on her arm that bound them as mates.

She wouldn't be unconscious.

He jumped to his feet with a growl and paced. He told himself she was fine. Her body was just recharging. But his thoughts carried too much doubt to believe any of it. As a youngling, he'd never overtaxed himself while using magic. Even as a King, he hadn't brought himself to that brink. He hadn't thought it was even possible.

The proof, however, was Lotti's comatose body. She had suppressed and stifled her power for nearly three hundred years. And in a very short period of time, had embraced her magic and learned she was one of the Star People. From that moment, Lotti had been relentless in pushing the boundaries of her abilities.

Alasdair rubbed his chest as he paced. He never wanted to feel this way again. If he had his way, he'd put Lotti somewhere no one could hurt her. How many times had he rolled his eyes when he heard one of the other Kings talking about worrying over their mates? Alasdair hadn't understood their feelings. Now, he did. He owed each of them an apology.

To find the person meant to be yours was a wonderful, terrifying thing. It made a person feel indestructible. He felt like he could do anything, *be* anything. He could conquer his worst enemy. He could right every wrong. He was a better man because of Lotti.

There was a flip side that none of his brothers had spoken about, though. At least not to him. The dark side of love. Where he realized how fragile and delicate life was. Where he worried about every little thing.

Where he looked at the world and things in it with varying degrees of trepidation because something could rip Lotti from him.

He pivoted and found Cullen in the doorway. Alasdair stalked to him, his frustration barely leashed. "Why did no one tell me? Why did none of you ever talk about how difficult it is to deal with the fucking terror?"

"What would be the point?" Cullen replied.

"I bloody hate when you answer a question with a question."

Cullen's pale brown eyes met his. "It's part of loving someone. Our mates feel the same fear we do."

Alasdair swung his head to the bed. "I hadna considered that."

"I didna either. Tamlyn was quick to make me see."

There was a smile in his voice that had Alasdair looking at his friend. "How do you do it?"

"The same way we dealt with losing our dragons on Earth. Minute by minute, day by day. Some days are easier. Then there are times like these, and I can no' even think of Tamlyn being mixed in the battle the way Lotti and Jeyra were." Cullen's stare intensified. "But know this, brother. If there is a war, Tamlyn will demand to play a part. Regardless of what I think or how I feel about it. And I willna stop her. Just as you willna prevent Lotti."

"You sound verra sure of that."

Cullen shrugged and leaned against the doorway. "Because I am. Life is dangerous no matter where we live. You know this, Alasdair. Your fear is clouding your thoughts. You're no' a man who shuts his mate away in hopes she won't break a nail. You're a King who gained Lotti's trust and showed her that magic could be useful. You gave her the confidence to stand on her own against powerful enemies."

"That was before I knew what it was to love her—and almost lose her."

"No' true. You loved her when both of you looked for Merrill. You loved her when you fought the soldiers and Villette. You almost lost her then, and you didna act the fool."

"Then why now?" Alasdair demanded.

Cullen's lips flattened. "Your no' going to like it."

"I have no' liked much of what you've said."

There was a ghost of a smile on Cullen's lips. "It's because the invisible being attacked you and knocked you out. For the first time in your life, you were no' the one to save others. Varek was also attacked and knocked unconscious. Both of you were at its mercy. The bastard has an affinity for Kings, apparently. The point, however, is that Lotti had to do most of it on her own. You were no' there beside her as you usually are. And your thoughts are on a loop of all the ways things could've gone wrong."

All the fight went out of Alasdair when he realized Cullen was right. "How do you know that?"

"Because I've been thinking it. So has Varek. So will all the other Kings with mates. The *what if?* What if we've finally encountered something that can kill a Dragon King? What if our magic can no' destroy it? What if we die, taking our mates with us?" Cullen blew out a breath. "Things went our way this time because of Lotti. Aye, brother, I understand your distress because I would be exactly where you are if our places were switched. But you might want to reconcile all of this before she wakes. Because she will."

"Again, you sound so certain."

"I'm willing it to be. You might want to try that instead of your current thinking."

Alasdair leaned against the doorframe and briefly closed his eyes. "You should've seen her. She was incredible. She never gave up. No' even when she knew she couldna hold the shield forever."

"The two of you share that. Neither of you knows how to quit."

"That could be said for all Kings." Alasdair rubbed the back of his neck. "We do have one advantage, though."

Cullen's brows lifted. "What's that?"

"Lotti can see the entity."

A slow smile curved Cullen's mouth. "That we do. Varek drew what he was able to see when you rained fire upon it."

"Lotti will give us more details when she wakes."

"Aye." Cullen slapped him on the back. "All will be well, brother. You'll see."

Alasdair waited until Cullen walked away before returning to his chair. He took Lotti's hand in his. Cullen was right. It wouldn't do anyone any good for dark thoughts to consume him. Alasdair knew where that led, and he didn't like who he became when he was like that.

The woman who had his heart, the one he loved with every fiber of his being, had saved the day. She'd shown everyone just what she was made of, and it was impressive as hell. Her life had done a one-eighty in a short time, but she had taken it all in stride. He would always worry about something happening to her, just as she probably would with him. But they were warriors fighting against tyranny.

Not everyone could fight. There were also those who could but wouldn't. Then there were those like Lotti, like the Dragon Kings, and their allies. They were the ones who stepped forward, freely putting their lives on the line for others.

Alasdair knew he had much to learn about handling his fear of losing Lotti, but all he had to do was look at her to remember they might each be good on their own, but they were an unstoppable team when together. It was about more than their magic. It was about their love for each other and their extended family.

"It's time to wake up, love," Alasdair whispered. He brought her hand to his lips and kissed her knuckles. "You've kept me worrying long enough. We're home and safe now. Because of you."

Alasdair gently replaced her hand on the bed and began thinking over the shackles and netting. He and Varek were the only two who had experienced both. The netting had been sticky, like a spider's web. The threads strong but pliable. They weren't easy to break. And something on the strands had impeded his magic.

The shackles were the same. As soon as they had locked around his wrists, they weakened him. Like walking in thigh-deep tar. Those on Zora who feared and hated magic made sure they had a way to keep others from using theirs. And if they could do that, then there was a way to block those items and any others. The Kings needed to figure out how to do that. They had few allies on Zora, but it might be time to reach out to the ones they had.

But first, they needed samples of the net and shackles.

Chapter Nineteen

The sound of Alasdair's voice pulled Lotti from sleep. She stretched and frowned. His voice sounded distant. She tried to open her eyes and had to blink several times before she could see clearly. A sigh fell from her lips when she realized she was in their bedchamber. That meant they had gotten away from the entity.

Once more, the sound of his voice reached her. Lotti looked around the room, but he wasn't there. Then she saw him walk past the door, patting Ben on the back. The baby let out an impressive burp that had Lotti grinning.

"That's a good lad," Alasdair said softly. "Let's try no' to eat quite so fast this time, or I'll have to burp you again."

Lotti sat up and scooted against the headboard, waiting for Alasdair to walk past again. He no longer spoke. Instead, he hummed while Ben slurped loudly on a bottle.

"I'm beginning to think the idea of eating slow doesna register," Alasdair mumbled.

Lotti's heart skipped a beat when he glanced into the room and halted when he spotted her. A slow smile curved his lips. She didn't think she could love him more than she already did, but somehow it happened. Maybe it was the way he stared at her as if she were the best thing he had ever seen. It could be seeing him holding Ben so lovingly. It might be because they had survived another encounter with their enemies.

It was likely all of it.

"I doona mind telling you that you scared me to death," he said as he walked to the bed.

She jerked her chin at Ben. "Can I hold him?"

"Of course."

She put one of the pillows beneath her arm, and Alasdair gently handed the baby over along with his bottle. Lotti stared down at Ben's cherubic face. She felt a tug at her heart when his tiny fingers wrapped around one of hers and squeezed as he continued to eat.

"Lotti?"

Her gaze lifted to find Alasdair's face near hers. Their lips met for a lingering kiss before he leaned back and stared at her with his sherry-colored eyes. She saw the fear he couldn't quite hide. "I'm all right," she assured him.

He kissed her forehead before sinking into the chair beside the bed, one she realized he probably hadn't left often. But that was the type of man her mate was.

"Really?" he asked.

"Aye. I feel rested."

"No injuries?"

She shook her head. "None."

He sighed. "You've been unconscious for a full day."

"I see." She drew in a breath and released it as she returned her attention to Ben. "My memory is fuzzy. What happened?"

"You kept the shield up until the being cracked it."

"I should've been able to keep the entity out longer."

Alasdair leaned forward to rest his elbows on his knees. "Doona do that, love. It was an exhaustive day for all of us. You repeatedly used powers you're still learning."

"But what good are they if I can't use them as I want?"

"You will."

She glanced in his direction. "I'd better. Otherwise, I'm useless."

"If it were no' for you, there is no telling where any of us would be."

"Maybe."

"Lass, you can see the enemy. We can no'."

She removed the empty bottle from Ben's mouth and lifted him to her shoulder to gently pat his back. "How did we get home?"

"Varek and I saw where the thing was battering your shield. We waited until it collapsed, then shifted before engulfing it in fire. I saw the outline of it flopping around for a wee bit, but it got away."

"Then you flew us home?"

"It returned."

Lotti frowned at Alasdair. "What? Where are Varek and Jeyra?"

"They're fine. It went after Jeyra's pack."

She briefly closed her eyes. "When I fell unconscious, the magic stopped. Shite."

"The entity was intent on the stone, no' Jeyra. That gave her the time she needed to get the straps off her arms and get to Varek. Then we burned it again."

"Is it dead? Did you kill it?" she asked excitedly.

Alasdair's lips twisted ruefully as he sat back in the chair. "I doona think so. However, one thing *is* gone. The stone. Our fire melted it."

"Well, at least we don't have to worry about it falling into Villette's hands again."

"It would've been nice to use it."

She adjusted Ben on her shoulder and realized he had fallen asleep. "Maybe. I have a feeling it's better that it's gone so no one can use it."

"Let me have the bairn. I'll put him down. I bet you'd like a long bath and some food."

"Aye to all of that," she said with a smile.

Lotti was careful not to wake Ben as she handed him off to Alasdair. Then she stood, feeling a slight stiffness throughout her body. She probably should've held off assuring Alasdair that she was fine until she'd moved around. He saw her wince and raised his brow in silent question.

"Nothing a bath won't fix," she said. Then she waved him off. "Go now, before you wake Ben."

He flattened his lips but did as she requested. Lotti filled the tub with hot water and used the time to walk around the chamber and test her body. Other than the minor stiffness, she did feel okay. She had a lot more training to do because she knew their enemies wouldn't give up. And if her encounter with Villette had shown her anything, it was that she had a lot to learn.

Alasdair returned with food. He closed the door behind him and set the tray on the small table near her. Then he undressed. She grinned, never taking her eyes off his impressive body as he stepped into the tub and slowly lowered himself into it, facing her. The water sloshed over the sides as his legs moved to either side of her. She laid hers over his.

"How do you feel, lass?"

She smiled, knowing the question had been coming. "I feel okay. I just needed to move around. I'm going to train harder now."

"I expected you would."

"You don't agree?"

He slid deeper into the tub until his head rested against the rim, and the water lapped at his chest. "I didna say that."

"What are you trying not to say?"

He flashed her a quick grin. "There's no harm in resting."

"We don't have time for that."

"Then we make time."

She shifted, the water sloshing over the side. "I'm capable."

"If there's anything I've learned in my verra long life, it's that there will always be some evil to fight. It's the time we take to savor the special moments that count."

Lotti studied him as she thought about how helpless and terrified she had been when he was unconscious. She sat up to look at the tray and chose one of the small sandwiches to hand to Alasdair before taking one for herself. "You're right. Villette isn't going anywhere. We won't know about the entity until we go searching. We have this time. Let's take it while we can."

"I thought you'd put up more of a fight."

She put a finger to her lips as she chewed then swallowed. "I need to train and expand my magic before I face Villette again. I need help with that. I want to reach out to Eurielle. She said she would give me answers. However, I kept thinking about one other thing during our mission."

"What's that?" he asked.

"You. Iron Hall. Everyone here. I know love now because of you. I have a home. People. I know who I am. I might still be figuring things out, but all of this is special. I could've lost it. Aye, when I woke, I had one thing on my mind. But then you reminded me of everything I hold dear."

His hand ran along her calf, over her knee, and up to her thigh. "You are everything to me, lass. You are my mate, my love, my home. I'll always be beside you."

"We make a good team."

He gave her a crooked grin. "The best."

She released a breath and lowered herself into the water until only her head was visible. Alasdair's gaze never left her. He was right about taking some time. It would be difficult for her, but it was also the right thing to do. She might not be training, but she could make a list of things she needed to learn.

After a moment, his grin widened. "You're thinking about training."

Lotti started to deny it, then shrugged. "I have a lot to catch up on."

"You might no' need to contact Eurielle. At least no' for training."

"Oh?"

"Rhi will return with Erith."

The goddess who'd created Zora for the dragons. "You really think she's one of my people?"

"We'll find out soon. She's powerful like you and the Star People.

Even if she isn't one of your kind, she might be able to help with your abilities."

"You think she would?"

Alasdair rubbed the arch of her foot. "Erith is one of the most giving people I know. Like you, she had a verra difficult beginning. I think she would be more than happy to help."

"If she comes."

"She'll come," he assured her.

Lotti finished her sandwich. "Erith's arrival might turn the tide of things. And not in a good way."

"I suppose we'll find out."

"Aye."

"That's enough of such talk," Alasdair said as he pulled her toward him.

Lotti issued a startled yelp that turned into a laugh. She found herself straddling Alasdair's lap. His hands slid sensuously over her bum to her waist and then to her back. Hunger filled his gaze as he sat up, bringing his mouth a breath away. He set her ablaze with that look.

She wound her arms around his shoulders. "Do you have something else in mind?"

He leaned her back until her breasts were thrust forward. His eyes never left her as he leaned in and swirled a tongue around a turgid peak. Then he said in a husky voice, "I'm sure you can figure it out."

Her eyes rolled back in her head as his lips closed around her nipple.

Epilogue

The next day...

Rain came with the dawn. A vicious thunderstorm that would keep anyone indoors. Anyone except a Dragon King, that is. It was during such tempests on Earth that the Kings took to the skies. Alasdair had resented that he couldn't fly whenever he wanted. He'd thought that would change on Zora—and as long as he stayed on dragon land, it had. He could. The storm made him think of Dreagan, though, the Kings' home in the Highlands of Scotland.

He missed the gray stone manor they had built. He missed the Dragonwood, their whisky, and his mountain he went to for solace. Things never looked simple in the moment. Now, looking back, they had been. He couldn't say the same for the current situation on Zora. And he feared it would be a very long time before he—or anyone else—could.

"What is taking so long?" Lotti murmured as she jumped up from her seat to pace.

Alasdair watched her as others filed into the great room with its arched doorway, as well as the impressive domed ceiling. There were rows and rows of chairs with an aisle down the middle that led to the front that had been left bare for the time being. Cullen had found it weeks ago. After Marcus used his architectural skills to fix the fallen walls and weakened ceiling, it had been declared a perfect location for the Kings to meet in private. It just so happened that Erith's impending arrival meant they now had an occasion to use the room.

Jeyra looked over at him and gave him a sympathetic smile. As soon as Lotti had learned of Erith's appearance, she became antsy. He shrugged, grinning at Jeyra. He knew Lotti well enough to know she would be fine once she met Erith.

The room buzzed with conversation. Alasdair spoke to the other Kings, catching them up on everything. Some were missing from the gathering. Merrill, for one. Nikolai was with his mate, Esther, helping the Skye Druids with something. Then there was Brandr, who had taken it upon himself to learn about the occupants of Zora. Evander was sweeping the northern border while Hector took the south. They'd bring them up to speed with everything as soon as possible.

A hush fell over the room. Lotti jerked to a halt, her gaze sliding to the doorway at the back. Alasdair rose to stand beside her. Eurwen moved to the front of the great hall and stood waiting with her mate, Vaughn. Constantine, King of Dragon Kings, strode down the center aisle. On Zora, he traded his expensive suits for more relaxed attire of slacks and a thin sweater. His black eyes swept the area before pausing on Eurwen.

Beside Con was Rhi. The royal Light Fae had her long, black hair down and unadorned. She wore a gold satin button-down tucked into black pants and impossibly high heels. She and Con wore smiles as they approached their daughter and Vaughn.

Only a few paces behind them was Erith and her mate, Cael. Alasdair hadn't spent much time with Erith or the Reapers, but he enjoyed what little he had. Cael, a former Light Fae, towered over Erith's petite frame. His black hair reached his shoulders, and his purple eyes saw everything. He glanced at his mate, their gazes meeting briefly. Erith's blue-black hair was in a fishtail braid that fell to her hips. She was dressed in her favorite color: black. She wore a boatneck shirt beneath a biker jacket, with jeans and boots.

Alasdair knew the instant Erith and Lotti spotted each other. The rest of the room vanished as the two walked toward one another. He wanted to be beside Lotti, but she didn't need him. She was capable of handling this on her own. Still, he watched. Just in case.

"You're like me. I can feel it," Lotti said. "You're one of the Star People."

Erith released a breath. "Then there is much we need to discuss."

Alasdair smiled when Lotti turned to look at him, her turquoise eyes shining with happiness. He didn't know what this meant for any of them, but they would find out soon enough.

* * * *

Merrill and the rest of the Dragon Kings will return in *Dragon Born*, coming July 2024.

* * * *

Also from 1001 Dark Nights and Donna Grant, discover Dragon Lover, Dragon Unbound, Dragon Revealed, Dragon Lost, Dragon Claimed, Dragon Night, Dragon Burn, Dragon Fever, and Dragon King.

Sign up for the 1001 Dark Nights Newsletter
and be entered to win a Tiffany Key necklace.

There's a contest every month!

Go to www.1001DarkNights.com to subscribe.

**As a bonus, all subscribers can download
FIVE FREE exclusive books!**

Discover 1001 Dark Nights Collection Eleven

DRAGON KISS by Donna Grant
A Dragon Kings Novella

THE WILD CARD by Dylan Allen
A Rivers Wilde Novella

ROCK CHICK REMATCH by Kristen Ashley
A Rock Chick Novella

JUST ONE SUMMER by Carly Phillips
A Dirty Dare Series Novella

HAPPILY EVER MAYBE by Carrie Ann Ryan
A Montgomery Ink Legacy Novella

BLUE MOON by Skye Warren
A Cirque des Moroirs Novella

A VAMPIRE'S MATE by Rebecca Zanetti
A Dark Protectors/Rebels Novella

LOVE HAZARD by Rachel Van Dyken

BRODIE by Aurora Rose Reynolds
An Until Her Novella

THE BODYGUARD AND THE BOMBSHELL by Lexi Blake
A Masters and Mercenaries: New Recruits Novella

THE SUBSTITUTE by Kristen Proby
A Single in Seattle Novella

CRAVED BY YOU by J. Kenner
A Stark Security Novella

GRAVEYARD DOG by Darynda Jones
A Charley Davidson Novella

A CHRISTMAS AUCTION by Audrey Carlan
A Marriage Auction Novella

THE GHOST OF A CHANCE by Heather Graham
A Krewe of Hunters Novella

Also from Blue Box Press:

LEGACY OF TEMPTATION by Larissa Ione
A Demonica Birthright Novel

VISIONS OF FLESH AND BLOOD by Jennifer L. Armentrout and
Ravyn Salvador
A Blood & Ash and Flesh & Fire Compendium

FORGETTING TO REMEMBER by M.J. Rose

TOUCH ME by J. Kenner
A Stark International Novella

BORN OF BLOOD AND ASH by Jennifer L. Armentrout
A Flesh and Fire Novel

MY ROYAL SHOWMANCE by Lexi Blake
A Park Avenue Promise Novel

SAPPHIRE DAWN by Christopher Rice writing as C. Travis Rice
A Sapphire Cove Noveal

LEGACY OF PLEASURE by Larissa Ione
A Demonica Birthright Novel

EMBRACING THE CHANGE by Kristen Ashley
A River Rain Novel

Discover More Donna Grant

Dragon Lover
A Dragon Kings Novella

Can she learn to love the man—as well as the dragon within?

Sensual. Clever. Daring. There's only one thing Kendrick yearns for—peace that has eluded the Dragon Kings. Zora may have been made in the image of Earth, but it's a far cry from home. For too long the Kings have been on the defensive, betrayed time and again. When Kendrick has an opportunity to stop a foe, he takes it. Except he isn't the only one tracking it. Soon, he finds himself face-to-face with an exquisite swordswoman who holds him enthralled...and sparks passion within his cold heart.

As an Asavori Ranger, Esha has dedicated her life to protecting her people. She trains relentlessly to become one of their best warriors, forsaking everything else. When a treacherous new enemy invades their lands, she vows to destroy it. Esha's rash decision has her crossing paths with that of a mysterious, handsome outsider. He's trouble the Rangers don't need, but she can't walk away. He awakens desires long buried and dreams neglected. The temptation of their forbidden union is more than she can resist. She's soon walking a treacherous path—one that could be the downfall for them both.

* * * *

Dragon Unbound
A Dragon Kings Novella

He's never been tempted...until her.

Sexy. Mysterious. Dangerous. He's an immortal Dragon King bound by ancient rules and eternal magic. Cullen has one objective: find and destroy the evil that threatens the new home of the dragons. Just when he's closing in, he's ambushed and finds a stunning warrior woman fighting alongside him. No amount of magic could prepare him for the beguiling lass who spurns his advances and defies him.

From the moment Tamlyn takes a stand against her kind, she's had to fight one perilous battle after another. Staying alive in an endless struggle, and the lines between good and evil are blurred with every encounter. She's always stood alone—until she comes to the aid of an irresistibly handsome stranger. Cullen will force her to face truths she's been running from...even as enemies plot to destroy them both.

* * * *

Dragon Revealed
A Dragon Kings Novella

The capture of a Dragon King is cause for celebration. Jeyra never dreamed she would actually face one of the creatures who destroyed her home. But the longer she's around him, the more she finds herself gravitating to him. All it takes is one reckless kiss that unleashes desires and the truth that has been hidden from her to set them both on a course that could be the end of them.

Varek, King of Lichens, has known nothing but a life with magic. Until he finds himself on a different realm unable to call up his powers. Worse, he's in shackles with no memory of how it happened. When he sees an enthralling woman who leaves him speechless, he believes he can charm her to free him. The more she rebuffs him, the more he craves her, igniting a dangerous passion between them. Can he protect the woman he's fallen for while uncovering the truth – or will peril that neither see coming tear them apart?

* * * *

Dragon Lost
A Dark Kings Novella

Destinies can't be ignored. No one knows that better than Annita. For as long as she can remember, it's been foretold she would find a dragon. A real-life dragon. She's beginning to think it was all some kind of mistake until she's swimming in one of the many caves around the island and discovers none other than a dragon. There is no fear as she approaches, utterly transfixed at the sight of the creature. Then he shifts into the shape of a thoroughly gorgeous man who spears her with bright blue eyes. In that instant, she knows her destiny has arrived. And the dragon holds the key to everything.

All Royden wanted was to find an item his brother buried when they were children. It was supposed to be a quick and simple trip, but he should've known nothing would be easy with enemies like the Dragon Kings have. Royden has no choice but to trust the beguiling woman who tempts him like no other. And in doing so, they unleash a love so strong, so pure that nothing can hold it back.

* * * *

Dragon Claimed
A Dark Kings Novella

Born to rule the skies as a Dragon King with power and magic, Cináed hides his true identity in the mountains of Scotland with the rest of his brethren. But there is no respite for them as they protect the planet and the human occupants from threats. However, a new, more dangerous enemy has targeted the Kings. One that will stop at nothing until dragons are gone forever. But Cináed discovers a woman from a powerful, ancient Druid bloodline who might have a connection to this new foe.

Solitude is sanctuary for Gemma. Her young life was upended one stormy night when her family disappears, leaving her utterly alone. She learned to depend solely on herself from then on. But no matter where she goes she feels…lost. As if she missed the path she was supposed to take. Everything changes when she backs into the most dangerously seductive man she's ever laid eyes. Gemma surrenders to the all-consuming attraction and the wild, impossible love that could destroy them both – and finds her path amid magic and dragons.

* * * *

Dragon Night
A Dark Kings Novella

Governed by honor and ruled by desire

There has never been a hunt that Dorian has lost. With his sights sent on a relic the Dragon Kings need to battle an ancient foe, he won't let anything stand in his way – especially not the beautiful owner. Alexandra is smart and cautious. Yet the attraction between them is impossible to deny – or ignore. But is it a road Dorian dares to travel down again?

With her vast family fortune, Alexandra Sheridan is never without suitors. No one is more surprised than she when the charming, devilish Scotsman snags her attention. But the secrets Dorian holds is like a wall between them until one fateful night when he shares everything. In his arms she finds passion like no other – and a love that will transcend time. But can she give her heart to a dragon??

* * * *

Dragon Burn
A Dark Kings Novella

In this scorching Dark Kings novella, *New York Times* bestselling author Donna Grant brings together a determined Dragon King used to getting what he wants and an Ice Queen who thaws for no one.

Marked by passion

A promise made eons ago sends Sebastian to Italy on the hunt to find an enemy. His quarry proves difficult to locate, but there is someone who can point him in the right direction – a woman as frigid as the north. Using every seductive skill he's acquired over his immortal life, his seduction begins. Until he discovers that the passion he stirs within her makes him burn for more…

Gianna Santini has one love in her life – work. A disastrous failed marriage was evidence enough to realize she was better off on her own. That is until a handsome Scot strolled into her life and literally swept her off her feet. She is unprepared for the blazing passion between them or the truth he exposes. But as her world begins to unravel, she realizes the only one she can depend on is the very one destroying everything - a Dragon King.

* * * *

Dragon Fever
A Dark Kings Novella

A yearning that won't be denied

Rachel Marek is a journalist with a plan. She intends to expose the truth about dragons to the world – and her target is within sight. Nothing matters but getting the truth, especially not the ruggedly handsome, roguishly thrilling Highlander who oozes danger and charm. And when she finds the truth that shatters her faith, she'll have to trust her heart to the very man who can crush it…

A legend in the flesh

Suave, dashing Asher is more than just a man. He's a Dragon King – a being who has roamed this planet since the beginning of time. With everything on the line, Asher must choose to trust an enemy in the form of an all too alluring woman whose tenacity and passion captivate him. Together, Asher and Rachel must fight for their lives – and their love – before an old enemy destroys them both…

* * * *

Dragon King
A Dark Kings Novella

A Woman on A Mission

Grace Clark has always done things safe. She's never colored outside of the law, but she has a book due and has found the perfect spot to break through her writer's block. Or so she thinks. Right up until Arian suddenly appears and tries to force her away from the mountain. Unaware of the war she just stumbled into, Grace doesn't just discover the perfect place to write, she finds Arian - the most gorgeous, enticing, mysterious man she's ever met.

A King with a Purpose

Arian is a Dragon King who has slept away centuries in his cave.

Recently woken, he's about to leave his mountain to join his brethren in a war when he's alerted that someone has crossed onto Dreagan. He's ready to fight...until he sees the woman. She's innocent and mortal - and she sets his blood aflame. He recognizes the danger approaching her just as the dragon within him demands he claim her for his own...

Rising Sun

Elven Kingdoms Book 1
By Donna Grant
Coming May 14, 2024

New York Times and *USA Today* bestselling author Donna Grant introduces a wickedly seductive new series with a ruthless, jaded elf and a bewitching human hiding a powerful secret—unlikely soulmates whose passion will test the boundaries of life and death.

* * * *

Chapter One

Rannora
Fall

Ravi glanced at the sign above the tavern that read Twilight. It was an upscale establishment in the Geggin Square district of Rannora. He stepped inside and was promptly enveloped by a sexy ballad coming from a star elf swaying her hips seductively on the stage as she held everyone within her thrall. Ravi took in the crowded business with one glance. His gaze swung to the left, nodding once to the stocky wood elf drying a glass behind the bar. The bartender returned the gesture. It was the only indication Ravi would get that all was well. And it was the only one he needed.

The sound of his bootheels striking the floor were drowned out by the singing. He weaved through the tables toward a side door where an elf stood to make sure no one entered who wasn't supposed to. As Ravi approached, the guard opened the door and let him through. The minute the door shut behind Ravi, the sounds of the tavern dimmed and faded as he continued down the narrow hallway. He didn't bother with any of the doors on either side of him. His gaze was locked on the one at the end of the hall.

He surreptitiously adjusted the sleeves of his leather jacket as he reached the door. Ravi paused for a moment to prepare himself before he knocked once. The door swung open immediately. He briefly looked at the muscled elf at the door before his gaze slid to the tall, slender occupant who waited within.

"About time," Durga stated with a brown brow raised, showing her impatience.

Ravi didn't bother to state that he was early. Durga had her own way of doing things, and the people she allowed to stick around were the ones who learned to roll with her particular method.

He walked to her, noting the navy dress that showed off her coppery skin that signaled her a wood elf. Intelligent, cunny hazel eyes studied him. Her brown hair was always pulled away from her face with nary a hair out of place and contained in a bun. The only thing that changed was the placement of the bun. Tonight, it rested at her nape.

"I take my summons to mean you have an assignment for me." Ravi had just finished another mission, but he was never good at sitting idle. Durga knew that. It was in everyone's best interest to keep him busy. It didn't hurt that he had never failed Durga or the Defense Intelligence Agency in his many years of service.

She eyed him. "I do."

Ravi studied his mentor more carefully. There were stress lines bracketing her mouth. She kept clenching and unclenching her hands at her sides. Wherever she was about to send him was going to be dangerous. "Tell me."

Durga cast a look at the other elf in the room. He quietly slipped out leaving just the two of them. Only then did her shoulders sag, letting him see just how anxious she was. "Do you remember when a dragon crossed our border?"

As if he could forget. It was all anyone had talked about for days. Some took it as a good sign while others took it to mean that their world was about to end. Ravi bowed his head. "Aye. Then it wasn't a rumor?"

"Rumor?" Durga snorted a laugh as she shook her head. "It was no rumor. We did have a dragon cross into Shecrish, but it wasn't just any dragon. It was a Dragon King."

"The Dragon King?"

"Nay. *A* King. There are many of them."

Ravi walked to the right to lean a shoulder against the wall as he digested that bit of information. "What did this King want?"

"To track down that thing that's been killing others. The one we can't see."

"We can communicate with dragons?"

"A Dragon King can shift from his true form to that of a human."

Ravi blinked in surprise. "Shite." All the years bordering the dragons, and one decided to seek them out. "Did he track down the thing?"

"Sadly, nay. Kendrick—that's the King's name—did make a few allies, however."

Ravi crossed his arms over his chest. "That means he also made enemies."

"Unfortunately. Made worse by the fact that one of our most distinguished Asavori Rangers fell in love with Kendrick and returned to his land with him."

He stilled. "Tell me she went willingly."

"She did."

"And you believe whatever source told you?"

Durga cut him a sharp look. "Three different sources shared that information."

That did make it difficult to easily dismiss. "I take it you want me to bring her home."

"Nay." Durga shook her head as she walked a few paces from him and swung around, her deep blue skirts swirling around her ankles. "Kendrick came to us in peace. He worked with Esha to—"

"Esha?" Ravi repeated as he jerked from the wall, his arms falling to his sides. "Are you telling me it was Esha who left with him?"

"I am."

Ravi ran a hand over his face. Asavori Rangers were revered by elves and humans in Shecrish. The Rangers were the first sent into any battle, and they usually were the only ones needed. Esha was known by all. Ravi had met her a few times when his missions brought him near the Rangers encampment in Flamefall.

"As I was saying," Durga continued. "Esha willingly worked with Kendrick. They tracked the thing slaying our people, and in return had a nightwraith sent after them."

Rave gave a shake of his head in surprise. Once the enormous creature had your scent, there was no getting away from it. "They survived?"

"Kendrick is a Dragon King with magic that exceeds anything elves have. He and Esha fought it in the forest where my people saw the entire battle."

Which meant Tarron, her cousin, and leader of the wood elves had been one of those who passed on the information to Durga. That was one source. Ravi wondered who the others were.

"It seems Kendrick's arrival stirred things up in the Conclave," Durga continued. "There is reason to believe someone on the Conclave sent the nightwraith after him."

For a long while, there had been those calling for a reform of their governing Conclave, but each time, it failed. Maybe now was the time to tackle that. "Tell me you know who is responsible. That crime needs to be dealt with immediately."

"That is being sorted out."

"By whom?" he demanded.

Her hazel eyes narrowed slightly. "I was going to give you that assignment, but another one has taken precedence."

Ravi waited, knowing that no amount of pushing would get her to give up the information faster. Durga revealed things in her own time. For someone who was known for her impatience, she didn't have a problem making others wait. But he was already trying to imagine what would be more important than discovered who tried to kill a Dragon King.

Durga gathered her hands at her waist and drew in a deep breath. "I received intel earlier about a group who intends to push us into war with the dragons by tossing an explosive across the border. You need to stop that before it can happen."

"Gladly. Where am I going?"

She hesitated. "That's the catch."

"You want me on this because you know I can get around anything. Nothing has stopped me before."

"I want you on this because you're the best agent we have, but there is a first time for everything."

"What aren't you telling me?"

"The location is deep within the Dangerous Peaks."

The only elves who dared to go anywhere near the snow-topped peaks to the east were the mountain elves who called them home. They were the finest weapons crafters, but they were suspicious of outsiders. Gaining their help would be difficult but not impossible.

"You know how reclusive they are. I'll need some time to find the mountain elves and gain their trust," he began.

Durga shook her head. "I wish it were that easy. There is no time to get help from our mountain kin. You have to get to Shaldorn Stronghold immediately."

"I've never heard of it."

"That is by design. Few know of it."

He frowned as he took a step toward her. "But you know of this place?"

"We've had our sights on it, aye. Getting in is another matter."

"I can get in."

"You can't." Then she went on before he could argue. "Shaldorn is a place where the vilest in Shecrish go to do despicable things. From what I've learned, they have anything there someone who walks in their circles could wish for."

Ravi shrugged. "I'll get in. There's always a way."

"There are two entries, actually. Both heavily guarded. It is a fortress, Ravi. The walls are too high to climb and watched by every angle. Only those with an invitation are allowed within."

"Then make sure I'm invited."

Her knuckles whitened as she gripped her hands tight for a heartbeat. "We tried."

That meant someone died. Ravi wanted to ask who, but he doubted Durga would impart that information. "So, how do I get in?"

"With the help of someone who has been inside. It has taken me all day, but I've had them found."

"What makes you think they'll return to this fortress?"

"I'm going to make sure they do." She motioned for him to follow. "We don't have long to get this mission underway. We should get there in time to see the individual brought to us."

Ravi followed her out of the room. The moment she reached the hall, two guards moved in front of her and another two behind him. No one spoke as they entered a stairway that took them outside. The four guards split up to stay hidden while Ravi remained just behind Durga. Only a fool would attempt to attack her.

"Ah. There," Durga said and pointed.

Ravi followed her finger. He spotted three undercover operatives. Then he scanned the faces of those milling around the shops set up on the street before he saw the human. She was a waifish thing of average height with black hair in a thick braid that reached the middle of her back. She walked with the steps of one who was ready to bolt at a moment's notice, her gaze moving about as if she expected someone to shout that she didn't belong. She stood out from all the finery in her worn black overcoat that had been mended so many times he couldn't believe it still held together, black shirt that had miss-matched buttons, and pants had a hole in the knee. And a strap across her chest connected to a bag. Her boots were old, but well take care of.

The human sidled closer to a female sun elf deep in conversation with another. Before the human could pick the elf's pocket, Durga made a motion with her hand. When she did, the operatives closed in around the woman. Ravi watched as she attempted to cradle the bag against her chest as the operatives grabbed her, but they yanked away.

The moment she lost the bag, the woman lashed out with everything she had. Instead of getting her quickly and quietly off the street, there was a commotion as everyone turned to look at the trio of elves attempting to subdue a human. The female never screamed or spoke, but she fought as if her life was on the line. And in a way, it was.

"This way," Durga murmured before she turned and retraced her steps.

They didn't return to the room. Instead, Ravi followed her down a flight of stairs that led underground. Fitting, since everything the DIA did was in the shadows. It was a clandestine operation that few beyond the Conclave knew existed. The Rangers might be who were called out in a fight, but the DIA were who the Conclave turned to before things escalated.

Ravi heard the scuffle before he saw it. The human female was so thin a breeze could blow her over, but she was quick. His fellow agents had her arms, but her legs and feet were free, and she used them efficiently. One of the men grabbed her hair and wrenched her head back. That didn't quell her. If anything, the human redoubled her efforts, managing to kick one of the men between his legs. That earned her a body slam against the wall just as yellow magic filled the palm of a sun elf as he readied to unleash it on her.

Durga cleared her throat. All three men seemed to remember they had an audience. They suppressed their need to lash out, but their anger was palpable. Humans didn't have magic, so for one to hurt an elf—worse, a female being detained—it made things worse. Their two cultures had always lived together, but the elves outnumbered humans twenty to one. Add in the fact humans were magicless, and there was always simmering contention.

The trio took the female into a room and shoved her into a chair so hard that it tipped backward. She jerked forward, just barely managing to keep from going backwards. The front legs of the chair banged against the floor as the human lifted her face and glared at the handlers.

Ravi and Durga stood outside in the hall watching her through glass crafted with elven magic that appeared to be a picture within the room. It allowed Ravi to get a look at the human. She sat up straight and settled as if she had come for a social visit.

He supposed she was pretty for a human. Oval face with full lips and a stubborn chin. Midnight brows arched over eyes a deep blue that reminded him of the ocean. Her size belied her strength, but it was her eyes that told him she had experienced things others could only guess at. She stared at the agents straight on, which told him she wouldn't cower easily.

It might be better if she did.

"Ready to meet your guide?" Durga asked.

Ravi's gaze jerked to her. "You're joking."

"You know me better than that."

He glanced back at the human. "She's…she's…"

"The only one that can get you inside."

"How can you be sure?"

Durga's gaze became icy. "If there was another way, I would've found it. The last thing I want is to bring an outsider, and a human at that, into this mission."

"She doesn't seem the type who will be willing to help anyone."

"She's doesn't have a choice."

Ravi blew out a breath. "Fuck."

About Donna Grant

New York Times and *USA Today* bestselling author Donna Grant has been praised for her "totally addictive" and "unique and sensual" stories. Her latest acclaimed series, Dragon Kings, features a thrilling combination of dragons, Fae, and immortal Highlanders who are dark, dangerous, and irresistible. She lives with an assortment of animals in Texas.

Visit Donna at:
www.DonnaGrant.com
www.MotherOfDragonsBooks.com

On Behalf of 1001 Dark Nights,

Liz Berry, M.J. Rose, and Jillian Stein would like to thank ~

Steve Berry
Doug Scofield
Benjamin Stein
Kim Guidroz
Chelle Olson
Tanaka Kangara
Asha Hossain
Chris Graham
Jessica Saunders
Stacey Tardif
Dylan Stockton
Kate Boggs
Richard Blake
and Simon Lipskar

Printed in Great Britain
by Amazon